DESPERATION

DARK ROAD – BOOK NINE

BRUNO MILLER

DESPERATION:
Dark Road, Book NINE

Copyright © 2021 Bruno Miller

Find out when Bruno's next book is coming out.
Join his mailing list for release news, sales, and the occasional survival tip. No spam ever.
http://brunomillerauthor.com/sign-up/

Published in the United States of America.

No rest for the weary.

With a second chance ahead of them and the moonshiner's compound in the rear-view mirror, Ben and his crew can resume their cross-country trek to Colorado. Or can they?

Three newly rescued acquaintances and another canine companion complicate their life on the road. And the addition of two more vehicles to their west bound convoy only adds to Ben's responsibilities.

Making matters worse, the open road quickly proves more hostile than they remember. Scarce supplies, extreme weather and desperate miscreants have made the landscape a living hell. They soon find themselves fighting for survival once again.

Ben's mettle and army training are put to the test in more ways than one, and he realizes it will take greater determination and cunning than ever before to stay on course. All while learning that help sometimes comes from the most unlikely places.

THE DARK ROAD SERIES

Breakdown

Escape

Resistance

Fallout

Extraction

Reckoning

Deception

Restitution

Desperation

· 1 ·

Ben started to recognize sections of the trail, and before long, the moonshiners' compound was nothing more than a distant plume of smoke rising into the air. After a few more minutes of driving and a lot of nervous glances in the rearview mirror, he found himself staring at the gate that had been his undoing. Now open, it mocked him and all he had been through. He signaled the others and brought the Blazer to a complete stop just on the downhill side of the gate.

"This will only take a minute." Ben hopped out of the truck and left the door open while he walked around to the rear. He unwound the heavy chain that had held the gate closed and threw one of the links around a tow hook on the Blazer. Next, he wrapped the other end around a section of the gate where it was bolted to the tree. Ben paused for a second, holding his side as he studied the connection, then looked down the line of vehicles.

Joel was leaning out of his window, trying to see what was going on.

Ben held up his finger. He didn't want anyone to get out here and make this into any more of a production than necessary. He climbed back into the Blazer and did his best to ignore his knee and ribs while inching the truck forward until the chain was taut.

Ben gave the old Chevy a little gas and watched the gate over his shoulder. At first, the wheels spun in the loose gravel until the aggressive tread on the oversized tires finally found purchase and bit into the dry, hard ground below. First one hinge and then the other popped off the tree, and with less effort than he thought it would take, the gate was torn free.

He let the Blazer drag the gate along the trail for a while until it was thoroughly twisted and bent. Satisfied he'd ruined it beyond repair, Ben braced himself to get out of the truck and unhook the chain, but Sandy stopped him.

"I got it." She touched his arm, slid out, and unhooked the chain, dragging it off the trail just far enough so the others could avoid running it over. Ben was hurt and tired and anxious to put some miles on the truck, but he wanted to make sure this detour road remained open for other travelers, should any be unlucky enough to find themselves here. If any moonshiners were left out there, they could easily drop another tree or build another roadblock, but it felt good all the same to destroy the one that had stopped him.

With the last of their ordeal behind them, he focused on the trail while keeping one eye on the others as best as he could. The route down was about the same as they'd experienced on their way up the mountain, except for a few steep sections that were more technical than he'd hoped to encounter.

They took turns spotting each other through the more challenging areas. Some areas were hardly big enough to squeeze through in the full-size Blazer, and there were times when Ben question whether they should go back and find another way. He couldn't stomach the thought, however, and they pressed on.

There were a few close calls, one being when the Toyota Allie was driving lost traction for a moment and slid into the side of a protruding boulder. She kept her composure, though, and other than a new pinstripe down the passenger side of the truck, she came out of the experience unscathed. Overall, Ben was impressed with her skill in navigating the rough terrain, not that he expected anything less from her. He was beginning to wonder if there was anything she wasn't capable of.

Martin, on the other hand, was a different story. In spite of constant instruction and reminders from the others to take it slow and easy, he seemed determined to test the truck's limits. Like a kid with a new toy, he was heavy on the throttle in all the wrong places. He swore he was doing his best to take their advice, but Ben began to wonder if the guy knew what "slow and easy" meant.

Despite Martin's inexperience with off-road driving, he still managed to get out of some tights situations, but Ben chalked a lot of it up to pure luck and counted himself fortunate the Scout was still in one piece. It took bottoming out on solid rock a couple of times and a slightly bent rear bumper to finally convince Martin to lay off the gas over the big rocks.

Eventually, he started to get the hang of it, but Ben assumed he only started listening to their advice because his kidneys were probably sore from all the bouncing. Thankfully, they'd packed the Scout tightly, and remarkably, all the gear seemed to stay in place, outside the occasional airborne backpack.

Ben was surprised by the difficulty of the trail, and there were times when it felt more like they were using a dry creek bed than a designated off-road-vehicle route. The heaviness of the overloaded vehicles didn't make things any easier, and even with his experience four-wheeling in the backcountry of the Rockies, some sections here gave him cause for concern.

One moss-covered boulder in particular caught

him off guard and put them all on the edge of their seats for a few tense moments. The Blazer was by far the heaviest of all the vehicles, and as soon as all four tires were on the damp, slick surface of the rock, they started sliding sideways down the incline. Ben was helpless as the blazer moved sideways, and it felt like they had hit a patch of ice. Fortunately, the ride only lasted a couple of feet and they stopped just shy of a large tree.

Ben directed the others to take a higher line over the sloped and moss-covered surface, making sure they kept at least two wheels in the dry dirt. The other trucks traversed it with no trouble, and they were back on their way without further incident.

The slow pace and unforgiving terrain were sapping whatever energy reserves they had left. Watching the time fly by wasn't encouraging, either. Ben was disappointed in their progress, and he'd hoped to be on the highway long before now. It was hard not to think they might have been well on their way if not for the two extra vehicles. But Ben tried not to dwell on that.

He snuck a peek in the rearview mirror and checked on Emma. At least she seemed to be in good spirits, all things considering. He wasn't crazy about adding another dog to the mix, but it was paying dividends right now with his daughter. Bajer couldn't have been any closer to her and had somehow managed to displace Sam at her side.

Eventually, the trail began to resemble a road more than a rockslide, and the steepness gave way to more gradual hills. They had to be getting close to the highway, but he was afraid to get his hopes up and wasn't going to get too excited until they saw pavement. A few minutes later, he spotted a break in the trees where the trail led to an access point for the road. They had finally made it.

Pulling out onto the blacktop was a feeling like no other. Only when he took the Blazer out of four-wheel drive did he truly allow himself to appreciate the fact that they had survived a situation many before them hadn't. He looked back at the other vehicles as they drove out onto the two-lane highway one by one and parked behind the Blazer. Ben limped around the truck, taking his time to check the tires and undercarriage after their off-road adventure down the mountain. All looked to be in good condition. He wished he could say he felt the same.

The others inspected their vehicles as well and made final preparations to hit the road. Allie joined Joel as he inspected the Scrambler, and Rita took her spot behind the wheel of the Toyota. Rita gave Ben a thumbs-up and buckled herself in as he walked past the couple and made his way to the Scout. He really hoped she was up for the drive ahead.

Ben joined Martin near the Scout and eyeballed the undercarriage for any damage. He gave it a thorough walkaround and found it hard to believe there wasn't a puddle of fluid under the truck. He certainly expected at least a leak of some sort, but the only damage was cosmetic.

"How's your knee?" Martin asked.

"Aw, it'll be all right. Just a little stiff." Ben hadn't been paying attention to how he was moving until now and immediately tried to limp less.

Joel and Allie approached, while Brad stayed in the Jeep with Gunner, probably afraid his dad was going to make him ride in the Blazer.

"That took a lot longer than I thought. I didn't think the mountains out here were this serious." Joel looked back up the dirt road.

"Yeah, that was pretty intense. I'm glad we all made it in one piece," Allie added.

"You guys did great. I was watching you both," Ben said.

"All except for this." Allie glanced over at the Toyota's damaged side panel.

"Hey, that's nothing. Look at this." Martin put one foot up on the Scout's newly curved bumper, like a trophy hunter over a kill. "Now that's a scratch." He laughed.

"It was definitely a good idea to leave the Cadillac." Joel lowered his voice. "Wouldn't have made it past the first switchback."

Ben agreed as Sandy approached and put her arm around her daughter and smiled. "Nice job driving."

"Thanks, Mom."

"So what's the plan?" Sandy asked.

"We drive until the first gas station we see, then look at the map and try to figure out a good place to spend the night. We're not going to get as far as I'd hoped." Ben shrugged.

"What if the first place we find for gas doesn't look good?" Joel asked.

"Unfortunately, I don't think we have much of a choice this time around. The Blazer's down to almost a quarter tank."

"Same here," Martin said.

"The Toyota has almost half a tank," Allie said.

"A little below half." Joel looked back at the Jeep. Gunner stood on the front seats, staring at them all curiously. Brad was watching, too, but he stayed mostly hidden behind the seat. Ben had the two five-gallon jerry cans, but when they were divided among the four trucks, it wouldn't make much of a difference. Better to save it if one of them ran out of fuel before they found a place to stop.

"Joel, are you still okay to have Brad ride with you? At least until we get out of the mountains," Ben asked.

"Yeah, no problem." He checked with Allie, who agreed with a nod.

"All right then, let's hit the road." Ben gave Joel a squeeze on the shoulder and headed for the Blazer.

He was tempted to make Brad ride in the Chevy with them but decided to let things stay as they were until their first fuel stop. It would be a tough sell anyway. Sitting in the back of a stuffy SUV with his sister and two large dogs versus riding in the back of the open Jeep with Gunner and hanging out with his big brother and Allie. There was no point in even bringing it up.

Besides, Ben didn't really want to upset the harmony in the Blazer right now, and if Brad was forced to do something he didn't want to, he would take it out on his sister. Ben was in too much pain and far too tired to listen to them argue for the next couple of hours.

He stopped at the Toyota for a moment, mostly to check in on Rita and Carlos before they started driving, but also to let Sandy get ahead of him. He didn't want her to notice how he was walking.

"You guys good?" he asked.

"We're all set." Rita showed him the piece of cardboard Allie had used to draw out the hand signals. She'd made one for Martin as well.

"If you have any trouble, don't be afraid to let me know. We're planning on stopping at the first place we see to get fuel."

The couple nodded, and Rita put her hand on Ben's as he rested on the door.

"Thank you," she said, patting his hand.

Ben smiled. "You'll be at your daughter's before you know it." He hoped that was true.

· 2 ·

Sandy was waiting for him at the driver's side door of the Blazer and blocked him from climbing in. "I don't think so. Let me take care of you for a change. Look at yourself. You can barely walk."

Ben sighed. She was right, and he was too tired to argue about it.

"Okay, but promise me you'll let me know when you need a break."

"I promise," Sandy agreed. Ben hadn't pictured leaving this place with Sandy driving, but he hadn't planned on being injured, either. Sitting in the passenger seat would give him a chance to work his knee a little so it didn't stiffen up as much as it would if he were driving. It would also give him time to study the map.

Ohio might be a bit ambitious for the amount of daylight remaining, but that wasn't their biggest obstacle. Lack of proper rest was the greatest threat to them right now. And even if they'd left hours earlier, they would still be limited by their stamina. They certainly weren't making it to Cloverdale today—or maybe even tomorrow, for that matter. What they needed was someplace safe and under the radar to spend the night and log some solid rest.

As Sandy pulled out and headed west, through the back window, Ben watched the caravan of vehicles follow. One big advantage to having Sandy drive would be his ability to keep an eye on the others. He thought Rita and Carlos would be his chief concern, but he found himself worrying more about Martin. The guy was still a little keyed up from their adventurous foray down the mountain, but that would wear off soon, and when it did, the monotony of the highway would take over. It was one of the main reasons Ben had wanted Joel to bring up the rear. It wasn't the best solution, but if Martin started to get tired and drift off the road, Ben hoped a few honks from the Jeep would be enough to wake him up and put him back on track.

Ben was tired as well, but he fought the urge to close his eyes. He didn't want to leave Sandy on her own. It wasn't because he didn't trust her with the job; he just knew she was as tired as he was. He also wanted to help keep an eye out for a gas station. Not too far up ahead was a town where they should be able to find fuel.

Ben noticed a sign for Treasure Lake and thought about Martin again. That was where he and his wife were headed before they were captured by the moonshiners. He was actually surprised at how well Martin seemed to be doing, considering all he'd been through. However, Martin might also be relieved that his wife would be spared all this, especially if she was already ill and suffering. Ben could understand that.

That was his biggest concern with Jack when they first arrived in Maryland. With his health, this would have been a hard trip on the old man. Jack might very well have suffered the same fate as Martin's wife if he'd been with them at the moonshiners' camp. In the long run, that would have been harder on the kids. Not that what happened was easy for them to deal with, but not much was these days.

Ben took a lot of comfort in knowing Jack died with the mindset that he'd protected the kids right up until the end. Going out like that, fighting, beat dying trapped in a metal container, helpless and worried about the kids. The longer Ben thought about it, the more he realized just how lucky they were to lay Jack to rest under the magnolia tree at his home. That was a luxury millions of people hadn't had since the morning the EMPs hit.

Ben felt himself slipping into a trance as he stared out the window. That was the worst part about not being behind the wheel: too much idle time to think. He could only stare at the map for so long. Not that he didn't dwell on things while driving, but it was a good distraction, and he could occupy his mind with navigating around the occasional wreck or crossing an overgrown median strip.

He turned to check on Emma and was glad to see her sleeping, along with both dogs. He hoped Brad was doing the same but doubted it.

"Good for her," Sandy said quietly.

"Yeah, she needs it. We all do."

"Why don't you try to get some rest?" Sandy asked.

"No, I'm not going to do that to you. Besides, we should be stopping soon. There's got to be a gas station at the next town." Ben eyed the map. "Looks like maybe twenty miles or less."

"Well, so far, so good. If the road stays like this, we should be there soon," Sandy replied.

"Let's hope so." Ben leaned over toward Sandy slightly and checked the fuel gauge.

"At least it's mostly downhill. We should be fine, right?"

"Yeah, I think so." Ben tried to sound more confident than he felt. But out of all the vehicles, he was most concerned with the Scout. Those after-market, high-performance parts he'd spotted under the hood weren't there for fuel efficiency; they were meant for horsepower gains. And that meant making sacrifices when it came to fuel consumption. The aggressive, thirty-eight-inch tires wouldn't help any, either. All that combined with Martin's heavy foot and undeniable fascination with hearing the big V8 engine roar made for trouble.

The only thing keeping Ben's anxiety in check was the fact that they had two spare cans of fuel. Of course, he didn't want to use them both on the Scout, and he didn't want to stop before they reached a place where they could all fuel up.

The guy had been through a lot, and Ben was grateful for him driving the rest of the supplies to Cloverdale, but he'd have to talk to him about his driving habits when they stopped. Ben cringed a little every time he heard the Scout's straight pipes over the Blazer's exhaust. He noticed Martin doing a lot of speeding up and slowing down in the old International, as well as some excessive side-to-side movements. Maybe the truck was too much for him to handle.

Relieved to see the sign for Falls Creek ahead, Ben felt some of his stress slip away. There had to be a gas station here; it was the first place they'd seen in over an hour. Then, a little farther down the road, he saw what they were looking for.

Sandy pointed. "Look, a sign for gas."

"It's not what I was hoping for, but we might not have a choice." Ben watched as the bright blue highway sign grew closer: *EXIT 97.*

He could barely make out the red and white Pilot Flying J Center logo through the overgrown weeds. They'd stopped at one of those on their way east.

"Take the exit?" Sandy asked.

Ben nodded. "Yeah, I guess so." He would have preferred if the gas station were directly off the highway, but it wasn't, and they needed fuel now. Ben heard Sandy tapping the Blazer's door as she signaled to the others that they were stopping. He was impressed she remembered the signal, although it was unnecessary this time. Ben took the radio from the console while waiting for Joel to pick up on his hand signal to contact them.

"Stopping for fuel? Over," Joel's voice crackled.

"Copy that. It's not ideal. We're gonna have to go into town a little way to get to it. Be ready for anything and tell Brad to stay low. Over." Now Ben regretted letting his younger son ride in the Jeep.

They had no idea what they were getting into, and Brad was exposed in the back of the Scrambler with nothing but gear to hide behind. And Gunner. Sandy glanced over at Ben when he pulled out the AR-15 and held it across his lap with the muzzle pointed out the window. Her concern didn't go unnoticed.

21

"Just in case," Ben said.

Sandy nodded and continued cautiously around the exit ramp. She knew the drill; they all did. It just seemed too soon—too soon to face another dangerous situation after what they'd just been through. Ben glanced back at Emma, who continued sleeping, half covered with dogs. It was the safest place for her right now, and with any luck, they'd fuel up and be out of here before she even knew they'd stopped, although he wasn't naive enough to think that would actually happen.

· 3 ·

Falls Creek looked as ruined and broken as any other place they'd seen in their travels. Ben didn't really expect to find anything different here, but a part of him always held out hope they'd discover another Cloverdale. He'd happily settle for a place with people who simply didn't want to kill them. But in their condition, he'd be just as satisfied to see a deserted main street that showed no signs of activity.

Sandy pulled wide around two black, scorched cars, a result of the EMPs and the subsequent head-on collision between them. The scene wasn't a new spectacle by any stretch of the imagination, but it still caught Ben's attention. There was no escaping the constant reminders of the world they were living in.

Some days were harder than others, and today was no exception. Ben noticed how easily distracted he was by common sights. He'd been dwelling on things more than normal on the ride, and he attributed that to his fatigue. He just needed to hold it together a little longer. Maybe a couple more hours on the road and they could all rest. He tried not to think about sleep; it just made the task at hand seem more difficult. It was going to take more effort than usual to fuel up with four vehicles and three extra people to keep tabs on.

Although he didn't anticipate Rita or her husband being too hard to keep track of, he also couldn't count on the older couple to help with the fueling process, either. Ben didn't expect them to, but it didn't help alleviate his building anxiety.

No matter how smoothly they carried out the refueling process, they were destined to be here for a half hour or more. That was going to be the way things went for the foreseeable future, at least until they parted ways with their new friends.

As Sandy rolled up the entrance into the Pilot station, Ben tried to calculate how long it would take to top off all the vehicles. It normally took them fifteen to twenty minutes to fuel up the Blazer and Jeep. Of course, setup and breakdown of the pump and hose accounted for some of the time and wouldn't change regardless of how many vehicles they filled. But that was the only silver lining he could find in the whole scenario, and he quickly gave up trying to figure out how much this would set them back timewise.

He was too tired to think about it anymore and knew worrying wouldn't change any of it. They would have to pace themselves anyway; moving fast and trying to rush the process wouldn't be wise in this heat. He also intended on assigning someone to keep a lookout for trouble. That would allow them to breathe a little easier. The others might think it was overkill, given their desolate surroundings, but then again, after the morning they'd had, probably not.

The gas station looked similar to the other shops and restaurants they'd passed on the way into town. The ones that weren't burned down, anyway. No glass, no doors, nothing but an empty shell of a building, picked clean by looters long ago. In a way, it was comforting to know there was nothing of any value here, and therefore, there was no reason for anyone to be around. That was what Ben hoped, anyway, as Sandy made their customary circle around the perimeter of the property and they scouted the place for any sign of trouble.

"And there goes Martin." Sandy snorted as they watched the Scout come bounding into the parking lot and pull right up to the gas pumps.

"I wouldn't be surprised to see him hop out and head inside for a coffee." Ben shook his head and smiled.

"He's got a lot to learn, doesn't he?" Sandy

looked away as she continued around to the backside of the building.

"Yeah, he does. I'll have a talk with him. I was planning on it anyway. If he keeps driving his truck like it's a race car, we're gonna have problems down the road." Ben kept his eye on the back door of the building and a small fenced-in area near a dumpster while Sandy finished her loop around the place.

"Well, what do you think?" Sandy glanced around the property.

"Do we have a choice?" Ben asked.

She checked the fuel gauge. "Not really."

"It looks fine, but let's be on our toes just the same." Ben located the bank of fill pipes for the underground fuel tanks and pointed them out. "Over there."

Unlike Martin, the others followed Sandy around the property and pulled in next to the Blazer as she parked in a small patch of shade created by an overhead billboard at the edge of the property.

"Is this good. Can we reach from here?"

"Yeah, I think so." Ben opened his door as she killed the engine.

"Where are we?" Emma yawned. The dogs had ruined her nap now that they were awake and whining with anticipation about the pit stop and the chance to get out of the truck.

"We have to get gas. You can get out and stretch your legs if you want. Maybe make sure the dogs don't get into any trouble." Ben barely got the words out before Sam jumped the center console and shot out through the open door. Bajer's approach was slightly more timid but just as direct. Ben was forced to put all his weight on his bad knee as he stepped back to avoid the dogs' hasty exit and was reminded very quickly of how sore he was. There was no way he could go chasing after the dogs if they got into something here.

"I'll help." Ben was surprised at Emma's willingness to participate, especially since she'd just woken up from a nap. It wasn't like her, and he wondered if the run-in with the moonshiners had given her a new outlook on things. Knowing you had cheated death was a liberating feeling, a feeling Ben was all too familiar with but one he wished the kids didn't have to experience.

But this was all new to Emma and Brad. Other than the incident with the two would-be thieves at Jack's, his youngest two hadn't been exposed to evil anywhere near the likes of what they'd just escaped.

"Now that's just cruel." Joel walked around to the front of the Jeep and laid his AR-15 on the hood while staring up at the billboard that was providing their shaded oasis. It was a Starbucks ad for some over-the-top iced coffee of some sort, complete with a towering pile of whipped cream and loads of ice inside a cup dripping with condensation. Ben was never a fan of the place, but he had to admit, the drink in the picture looked refreshing. Meant to lure travelers off the highway at this exit, the sign now stood like a beacon, reminding them of times past. The destroyed coffee shop across the street from the gas station proved it.

"I don't even want to look at it." Allie climbed out of the Jeep and made way for Gunner, who was anxious to join the other dogs in their exploration of the parking lot. Brad found his own exit from the Jeep and climbed over the side, using the tire as a foothold.

"It's so hot here, even in the shade," he moaned.

"Get some water. We all should while it's still cool," Sandy instructed.

"What's he doing over there?" Allie glanced over at the Scout.

"I have no idea, and neither does he. Joel, you want to get started? I'm going to go talk to Martin for a minute." Ben thought the guy would've put two and two together and joined them by now.

Joel nodded and started to gather what they needed to refuel. Ben grabbed a water bottle and his M24 from the truck before heading toward the Scout, which was nearly halfway across the parking lot. He struggled to walk without showing too much of a limp and tried to convince himself the exercise would be good for his knee.

"How can we help?" Carlos shouted from the Toyota.

"Just rest up for the drive ahead," Ben said. "We've got it handled." Carlos looked like he was about to protest, but Ben didn't give him the chance and kept walking past the couple's truck as fast as his knee would allow. They wouldn't be any help to Joel, and it was more important for them to save their energy.

Looking back at the Blazer and the other vehicles, Ben was glad Martin had parked over here. The billboard wasn't casting a large enough shadow to shade all the vehicles at once. But more importantly, the Scout was in a good position to see down the road in both directions. From here, Ben could even glimpse a portion of the interstate.

Martin was standing outside the vehicle, basking in the shade of the fuel island canopy and staring at the closest pump when Ben reached him.

"How do we get the gas out?" he asked.

Ben tried to remember this was the guy's first dose of the new reality they lived in and probably his first time pumping gas since the EMPs hit.

"We don't, at least not from here. We've got a system using a hose and a hand pump to pull the gas from the underground holding tanks. Joel can show you how it's done so you can help fuel the Scout when it's your turn."

"Want me to pull over there?"

"Might as well leave it parked in the shade here until the other trucks are done. Then you can trade places with someone. Go head over and see how it's done. I'll stay here and keep an eye on things. Tell Joel to leave the Blazer, will you? I can handle that."

"Okay." Martin turned and started walking away.

"Hey, don't forget your weapon," Ben reminded him before he was able to get too far.

"Oh, I mean...do you think we need them here? Seems quiet enough." Martin lifted his shoulder in a half shrug as he looked around.

Ben's eyes widened. "Looks can be deceiving. Trust me on that."

Without another word, Martin nodded and retrieved his AR-15 from the Scout while Ben set up his rifle across the hood, facing the interstate. He still needed to have a word with Martin about his driving skills, or lack thereof, but figured he better wait until after they fueled up. He didn't want to come off as too bossy. They needed him, and he was probably doing the best he could. This was a lot for anyone to take in, let alone a malnourished guy who'd just lost his wife and spent the last two weeks or so locked in a cage.

Ben used his scope to study the interstate before turning his attention in the other direction. The road that led them to the gas station continued on for another mile or so into a more congested area of town before separating at a four-way intersection. The only movement came from an occasional piece of trash blown across the street by a hot, dry breeze, which Ben hadn't noticed until now.

He continued his observation through the scope for a few more seconds, running the optic up and down the sides of the street, checking the smashed and burnt-out storefronts for any signs of life. Satisfied for the time being that they were alone, he relaxed his eyes and leaned against the truck. The metal was still hot from the sun, but it felt good to take some weight off his knee.

The cracks in the pavement under his feet were brimming with weeds. It was happening out on the main roadways as well. During their travels here today, he'd spotted several tufts of vegetation sprouting up through the pavement. They were only a few inches tall, but nature was beginning to reclaim what was once hers, something that was impossible with traffic constantly running over the surface just weeks ago, but not anymore. It was anybody's guess when the last vehicle had come through here.

The overgrowth along the roadways was well past completely covering some of the smaller signs now, and the mile markers had disappeared altogether. The highway sign that led them to this gas station was barely visible through the tall grass.

It amazed him how fast things were growing in this hostile environment. How long before nature reclaimed the roads to the point where they were nothing more than glorified trails? Would it actually come to that?

· 4 ·

Ben remained vigilant at his post until Martin and Sandy returned in the Blazer. She maneuvered the vehicle under the canopy and pulled in behind the Scout.

"She's all fueled up," Martin announced as he hopped out of the truck before Sandy came to a complete stop.

"I was going to help," Ben said.

"It's fine, no big deal." Martin headed right for the Scout.

"It was Joel's idea. You've done enough today." Sandy climbed down from the driver's seat of the Blazer.

"I'm perfectly capable of helping out if one of you wants to take my place here." Ben took his M24 off the hood of the Scout and slung it over his shoulder when Martin fired up the engine.

"It's fine. Relax." Martin smiled through the open window as he drove the Scout over to Joel, who was waiting with the fuel hose in hand. Ben waved at his son and nodded his appreciation for him taking the lead on this and getting it done. He felt guilty about not helping out, but it was nice to see Joel had it under control.

"Come on, sit in the truck and rest your knee," Sandy pleaded.

"I'm actually enjoying the breeze." Ben moved the rifle to the hood of the Blazer. "Besides, I can see better out here."

"Yeah, where did that breeze come from? It's been picking up steadily the last half hour or so." She looked up toward the sky. Ben noticed it, too. The horizon to their north was unmistakably growing darker by the minute. He'd been watching what looked like a sky full of heavy rain clouds in the distance but didn't want to get his hopes up.

"Oh, wow, I couldn't see that from under the billboard. I can't remember the last time it rained," Sandy added.

"It's been a while." As far as he could remember, they'd only seen rain twice on the trip so far. The more he thought about it, the surer he was. It was easy to believe. Nearly every area they had traveled through showed signs of drought. No wonder it looked more like the beginning of fall instead of late June. The only things that seemed to be thriving were the weeds and wild grasses sprouting up along the roadways.

The storm was a welcome sight for sure. The breeze it was creating, combined with the cloud cover, provided some much-needed relief from the scorching rays of the sun. The others noticed the darkening sky now as well and stopped pumping fuel to watch the storm build.

Joel looked back toward his dad and Sandy. "You guys see that?" he yelled.

Ben cupped his hands over his mouth and hollered back, "Yeah, you better wrap it up soon and get the top back on the Jeep." Joel and Martin went to work topping off the Scout while Allie and Brad started assembling the soft top panels for the Scrambler. Rita drove the Toyota over to the Blazer and pulled under the canopy for shelter.

Ben could make out flashes of lightning among the charcoal-colored clouds, and there was no doubt the storm was headed right for them. He hobbled over to the Toyota and checked the tarp covering the supplies in the back. Carlos managed to climb out of the truck and tried to help Ben cover the gear.

"It's going to be a big one. Should we wait it out here?" Carlos asked.

Rita stuck her head out the window and looked at Ben. "I'm afraid neither of us are very good at driving in the rain. Or at night, for that matter."

Rita's admission didn't come as a surprise to Ben, but he was planning on leaving as soon as the

Scout was fueled up and the Jeep was covered. He didn't like the idea of staying here any longer than they had to. The gas station was out in the open, and he felt exposed; they were vulnerable, and the longer they stayed in one place, the greater the odds they would find trouble—or, more likely, trouble would find them.

But what choice did they have? They were only as strong as their weakest link, and that link right now was Rita and Carlos. Ben had known this would be a factor but somehow imagined making it farther today before having to stop for very long. They still had a few hours of daylight left, and he really didn't want to spend it hiding from the rain.

Allie worked as fast as she could to get the soft top pieces for the Jeep organized and ready to zip into place, but even with Brad's help, they didn't beat the rain. As Joel and Martin finished fueling the Scout and began to put the equipment away, the big drops started to hit. Allie looked skyward for a minute and let the water splash on her face. It felt cool and refreshing. It hadn't rained in so long. Just the smell reminded her of better times.

She forced herself back to reality and realized if they didn't get this top put together fast, the gear was going to get soaked, and as good as the rain felt now, a wet sleeping bag would be no fun tonight. Just then, Emma ran by the Jeep, headed for the others under the shelter of the canopy. All three dogs were right behind her, but they didn't seem too concerned about getting wet, all except for Bajer, who ran straight to the Blazer. Gunner and Sam dawdled around a rain spout carrying a steady river of brown water out onto the parking lot.

"Why don't you join your sister? I'll pull the Jeep over and we can finish putting the top on out of the rain." Allie frantically ran around the Jeep and began picking up the soft top panels and throwing them in the back.

"Okay, but I can help you with this first." Brad joined her.

"It's okay. I got it. You're gonna get soaked," she squealed as a bright flash of lightning was followed immediately by the sharp crack of thunder. The rain seemed to intensify along with the lightning and began to fall extremely heavy now.

"I don't care." Brad wasn't giving in. But she wasn't concerned about him getting wet; they were all getting wet now. What she was concerned about was the lightning. What had started as subtle flashes of light contained inside the dark gray clouds had morphed very quickly into a full-blown lightning storm, the worst she'd ever seen.

"Hurry up! We need to get out of here," Joel shouted over the downpour and pushed Brad toward the shelter of the canopy as he ran around the Jeep to help Allie. They'd finished fueling the Scout, and Martin was already in the process of moving his truck to shelter.

Crimson bolts of energy licked at the ground in every direction as Joel helped her throw the last piece of the top in the back. Brad had taken his brother's advice and was long gone.

"Just leave it," Joel shouted.

"No, I can't. The gear will get ruined." Allie threw open the driver's side door and started to get in.

"Okay, I'll meet you over there." Joel took off running for the covered fuel island. Allie jumped behind the wheel, but before she could turn the key, the hair on the back of her neck stood up and a strange metallic taste filled her mouth.

Crack! For a brief moment, she thought the Jeep had been hit. Then sparks showered down from overhead. A lightning bolt had struck the metal frame of the billboard, causing the lights to energize briefly before popping like glass balloons. The mini explosions ignited the plastic sign material, but the rain was too heavy for the flames to gain a foothold, and the fire was soon extinguished.

Allie remained frozen in place as she stared up at the smoldering remains of the Starbucks advertisement.

"Allie, get out of there quick!" Ben's shouts brought her back to reality, and she started the Jeep.

"Allie, hurry up!" She could hear her mother's cries as she put the Scrambler in gear and stomped on the gas. The rear tires spun on the newly drenched asphalt but quickly found traction, launching the Jeep forward. The tires' grip on the wet surface was temporary, however, and when she cut the wheel too hard, the Scrambler hydroplaned sideways across the pavement a few feet. *Settle down. Come on, take it easy.*

Allie tightened her grip on the steering wheel and took her foot off the gas until she regained control of the Jeep. She let the vehicle's momentum carry her under the canopy and finally joined the others.

"That was close." Joel ran to the Jeep before she could get out and stood at the driver's side window.

"Too close." Allie turned off the engine and sat still, trying to catch her breath. She hadn't done anything that physically demanding but found herself struggling to breathe.

"You okay?" Joel asked.

"Yeah, I think so," Allie panted. Joel stepped back as she opened the door and slid out of the seat, onto the ground. She held both hands out in front of her body and watched them tremble uncontrollably. "Just a little shook up."

Sandy blew out her cheeks and exhaled a sigh of relief before running to Allie's side and wrapping her arms around her daughter.

"I'm okay, Mom. I'm okay."

· 5 ·

"I've never seen anything like it in my life."
Martin stood at the edge of a mini waterfall, the
result of a failing gutter on the canopy. The cascade
of overflowing rain slapped the blacktop loudly,
pushing waves of dirty water out across the
pavement. Ben watched as a couple weeks' worth
of dust and debris floated past the fuel island on its
way out to the storm drain in the street. The drain
was already starting to back up, clogging quickly
with an assortment of trash caught up in the small
river. One by one, the others joined him at the edge
between wet and dry and watched what he could
only describe as otherworldly.

Martin had summed it up well. This lightning
storm was unlike anything Ben had ever seen,
either. The colors of the bolts reminded him of the
red found in old neon bar signs. The intensity of
some of the strikes was both amazing and
frightening at the same time.

In his day, Ben had witnessed some pretty nasty high-elevation storms while hiking the San Juan Mountains, but all of them put together paled in comparison to this unbelievable display of power. He'd never witnessed lightning scatter and split off into so many fingers as it made its way down to the ground. It was like the air itself was electrically charged, and for every bolt of lightning that flashed, dozens more fractured off.

Except for the strike that hit the billboard, it seemed as though the worst of the storm was still north of them and looked like it might miss them by a few miles. Ben was thankful for this and wondered how safe they would be under this canopy if it did come this way.

Sandy broke the silence as they all looked on in amazement. "It's a good thing we're not driving in this."

"At least it's moving fast." Ben had hoped to be back on the road by now, but he was glad they hadn't been caught in this. If Rita was nervous about driving in the rain, she never would have made it through this storm. The rain was coming through in waves, and at times, the storm would have been impossible for any of them to navigate through, at least with any efficiency. And with four vehicles in the caravan, the chances of an accident in this slop were even greater.

Unfortunately, the storm looked to be moving west. Even after it passed, there was a chance they would catch up to it, and at the very least, it was going to soak everything along the route they needed to travel. Ben thought about how this would affect their night. Camping over wet ground was never fun, and packing up wet gear in the morning was even less enjoyable, in his opinion.

He already had his doubts about Rita and Carlos spending the night in a tent. They could likely do it, but what kind of shape would they be in for the drive the next morning? On this trip, Ben had spent his share of nights with nothing more than a sleeping pad between his sore back and the hard ground. The older couple had a good twenty-plus years on him and Sandy. He could only imagine how hard sleeping on the ground would be on their bodies. Then again, how much worse could it be than sleeping on the metal floor of a shipping container?

Eventually, the intensity of the lightning began to wane. As did everyone's interest in the storm. The kids wanted to go out in the rain now that the danger had passed, but Ben didn't think it was a good idea. With the air quality being what it was, he worried about the rain being toxic. He didn't want anyone exposing themselves more than necessary, and he certainly didn't want the dogs drinking it.

The air was still thick and loaded with God knew what. The pollution was most visible at sunrise and sunset. The smog-like effect that hung low in the sky wasn't normal and was undeniably one of the lasting effects of the EMPs. Ben couldn't help but think there had to be a lot of pollution in the rain.

Sandy agreed with him and thought it best to stay out of the rain as well. With the kids' plans for an impromptu shower thwarted, they soon lost interest in the storm and congregated around the Blazer's tailgate. Allie pulled out MREs for everyone and passed them around. It was a good idea to eat while they were stuck here, and maybe by the time they were done, they could move out.

Ben took the opportunity to study the map a little more. It wasn't that he hadn't been looking it over plenty already, but in light of the storm, they might have to reconsider their plans for the evening.

They were in Falls Creek, Pennsylvania, and if his calculations were correct, they would be approaching their nearest point to Pittsburgh in about an hour or so. Hopefully, this time they'd be far enough away not to see any of the effects of the bomb.

Last time they passed by Pittsburgh on I-70, they were heading eastbound and only about thirty miles away from what Ben figured was ground zero.

They would be twice that distance from the city this time, but he was still leery, especially about spending the night in the area. It was one thing to pass through quickly, but to linger somewhere there might be radioactive material from delayed fallout was something they needed to avoid at all costs. That might mean calling it an early day and camping on this side of any potential radiation hot spots. There were no guarantees with that, either, but it seemed to be a safer choice than the risk of sleeping on irradiated soil.

Finding a place to hold up for the night was beginning to look like something they would be doing sooner rather than later. The storm had let up, but the rain hadn't. Not yet, anyway. At least the system brought cooler temperatures and much-needed relief from the heat. Maybe they'd done enough for one day and should settle for finding someplace close and dry to sleep.

"How's it going?" Martin approached, carrying an MRE, his AR-15 hanging over his shoulder by the sling.

"It's going." Ben looked up from the atlas and surveyed the landscape beyond the gas station.

"How much farther do you think we'll travel today?" Martin asked.

"Honestly, I don't know that there's much point in going any farther. I don't want to spend the night too close to Pittsburgh. This whole area could be radioactive." Ben drew a circle with his finger on the map. The others had wandered over and were listening to the conversation now.

Carlos spoke up. "We're okay with stopping whenever you want." The comment didn't surprise Ben one bit, but it didn't help lessen the disappointment he was feeling about not getting farther away from the mountains. They'd been driving for less than two hours. If there were any moonshiners left and their desire for revenge was strong enough, Ben and the others could still be in danger.

Between the damage to the camp and the dead bodies they left in their wake, he could easily imagine any remaining moonshiners wanting to avenge their fallen and giving chase. If Ben and his group weren't going to travel any farther today, they at least needed to stay hidden. And the sooner they found a place to safely spend the night, the better he would feel.

The moonshiners weren't friendly the last time they met; he could only imagine how he would be treated if he was captured again. But he refused to think about that. Maybe he was just being paranoid. For all he knew, they had killed the last of the moonshiners with the dynamite. It was anybody's guess, and they would never know for sure. In his mental and physical state, he didn't feel like speculating on it anymore. And he certainly didn't want to worry the others with his thoughts.

Ben used the gas pump to pull himself to his feet. "Well, let's find a place to spend the night then. We could all use the rest."

"Camp? Around here?" Joel's forehead creased.

"Not exactly." Ben had been eyeballing an old motel a little farther into town. At first, he kept an eye on the place because it was suspect. The building was mostly intact, and he thought it was a likely place for people to take shelter, especially if they'd lost their houses when the EMPs hit. He hadn't spotted any signs of people living there, but that didn't necessarily mean anything.

However, the thought of sleeping on a mattress tonight was too tempting to ignore. They all needed a good night's sleep, something he was afraid wouldn't happen in the woods thanks to the rain. But the biggest reason he wanted to rest for the night was that driving in this weather would be slow going at best if they had to wait for Rita to keep up. This rain wasn't letting up, and the longer they sat here and waited, the greater the risk that someone would spot them. Trying their luck at the motel might be their best option right now. It wouldn't hurt to check the place out. At least he hoped not.

· 6 ·

The motel was about half a mile down the road toward the center of town. Driving this direction felt wrong; Ben's gut told him they should have been heading west on the interstate. But they had no choice. He was certain of that now as he watched Rita struggle to navigate the Toyota through the heavy rain. Ben kept an eye on the little pickup in his rearview mirror, making sure not to get too far ahead of the older couple. *She never would have made it on the highway.*

This wasn't the plan, but maybe this was a good thing. A real bed might be worth the trouble. And Ben was fairly confident they were alone. Nothing was guaranteed, though, and he'd given everyone a short speech about keeping weapons handy and staying alert before they pulled out from the gas station. While the others were fueling, he scoped this area out pretty well from the hood of the truck, and now he was glad that he had been so thorough.

No one said anything as they rolled slowly down the center of the street. Even the dogs were quiet and seemed to be watching for something out the windows. There weren't many buildings left standing; most of them had burned to the ground and were now little more than piles of rubble. Those remaining were nothing more than empty shells and had only survived because they were made of brick, stone, or concrete. On the right-hand side, they passed an electric vehicle supercharging station. The charging islands no longer stood upright. Their red and white plastic housings were melted and badly deformed from the EMP-caused power surge that fried them.

"Do you see those?" Sandy asked.

"Yeah, this place got hit pretty hard." Ben turned his attention to the motel; they were almost there. He pumped his brakes, hoping to give Rita plenty of time to react. The rain hadn't let up at all. In fact, it was coming down harder now than when they'd pulled out from under the canopy. Even with the wipers operating at full speed, he was having trouble seeing the curb cut to pull into the motel. The fact that there was a small flash flood coursing down the street wasn't making it any easier.

Ben was okay with the heavy downpour, though. If there was anybody around, it would most likely keep them inside.

"Sorry," Ben said, apologizing for the sudden jolt as the back tire caught the curb. He read the sign out loud. "Welcome to the Pinecone Inn."

"Gee, I hope they have a vacancy," Sandy joked half-heartedly.

"I don't think they'll mind if we check ourselves in." Ben eyed the motel office—or what was left of it. It looked like the place had initially caught on fire but for some reason didn't continue to burn. They'd have to force the doors open and dig through the remains of the office for room keys. As far as he was concerned, that wasn't an option in this weather.

They followed the exterior corridor of dark green doors to the back of the property, where the building made a turn. Ben pulled around to the backside of the motel and the rooms that faced the woods.

"This looks more promising than I thought." He turned and smiled at Emma while backing the Blazer into a spot directly outside the second-to-last room in the building. The others followed his lead, and one by one, they backed up to the adjacent rooms.

Ben turned the truck off and waited. "I guess it's not gonna let up."

"No, I don't think so. I can't believe how it's coming down. All this time with no rain and now this." Sandy leaned in and stared up at the sky through the windshield.

"Might as well get it over with, then." Ben threw the door open and stepped out into a couple inches of water. "If you want, you can wait here until I get into the room." He slammed the door behind him, trying not to think about the potential toxic cocktail of radioactive chemicals washing over him at the moment.

At least he could breathe easier out here, a welcome relief from the inside of the Blazer. Part of him was glad they weren't driving any farther. With the windows up to keep the rain out, the truck reeked of wet dog and who knew what else. On top of that, the glass was fogging up badly and making it progressively harder to see.

Moving as fast as his knee would allow, he ran around to the back of the Blazer and opened the truck.

"Sam, no!" Emma tried to stop the dog, but it was no use. Sam took the opportunity and jumped out of the truck. Bajer laid her head over the back seat and watched but was content to stay out of the storm with Emma. Sam ran under the covered vestibule and began sniffing her way along the row of doors while Ben retrieved the crowbar.

"Can I help?" Sandy joined him at the back of the truck.

"Maybe give Rita and Carlos a hand and keep an eye out for trouble. I don't think anyone else is here, but we can't be too careful."

"The rooms looked empty. I was checking as we drove past." Sandy adjusted the AR-15 on her shoulder and took a step up onto the covered walkway, out of the rain. Ben joined her after he closed the truck. Rita and Carlos were still sitting in their vehicle, but the others had found their way under the sheltered walkway. Gunner chased after Sam, who was already a few doors down by now.

"Not too far, Gunner, Sam," Joel called after the dogs.

"You think we'll be all right here?" Martin glanced around nervously.

"You want to camp in this?" Joel pulled at his dripping-wet T-shirt.

"It doesn't look too bad in there." Allie was at one of the windows with her hands up to the glass, looking in.

"It wouldn't take much to beat a wet tent." Sandy looked inside the room for herself.

"Be careful not to lean on that too hard." Ben pointed out the large crack running across the windowpane. All the windows were damaged but remained intact, unlike those on the front side of the building.

Ben didn't waste any time putting the crowbar to use and was able to pry open the first door much easier than he expected. Joel insisted on opening the other three, and Ben was happy to let him.

Meanwhile, Sandy and Allie braved the rain once more and helped Rita and Carlos move into one of the rooms.

Emma was finally able to coax Bajer out of the Blazer and help the others carry gear into the rooms. The kids decided they all wanted to stay in the same room. In an effort to avoid having to bunk up with her younger brother, Emma asked if she and Allie could share a bed, and Brad was more than happy to sleep with Joel. Ben was fine with the arrangement as long as they agreed to keep the door between the rooms open. He wanted to make sure they actually slept, although he doubted they had the energy for much else, but mostly because they were still kids. And as quickly as this world was forcing them to mature beyond their years, he wasn't about to let them out of his sight, even if it was just a door between them.

Having adjoining rooms would also allow the dogs to roam freely between the kids' room and theirs. Ben was counting on the dogs to be their early-warning system should anyone come snooping around the trucks overnight. He couldn't in good conscience ask anyone to stay up and stand watch. They were all at their limit. He would stay up as long as he could but knew the reality of the situation. No matter how hard he tried, he could only hold out for so long before his body gave in to the exhaustion.

At this point, he hoped the rain lasted all night. Maybe not this heavy, though; the parking lot was already flooded. He was thankful for the couple of steps up to the room, that was for sure. But the trucks would be fine, and he liked that they were hidden from the road on the backside of the property. With the motel looking so bad from the front, he doubted anyone who happened through would give the place a second look. That was what he was counting on, at least.

· 7 ·

Martin settled into the farthest room while Rita and Carlos took the room next to the kids. Sandy and Ben took the far-left room closest to the end of the building. Ben made sure the doors between their rooms and the kids' were wedged open.

"No, down. Come on." Ben heard Allie fussing with one of the dogs.

"Don't look at me. You're not coming up here all wet." Brad rebuked Sam's attempt to jump up on the bed he was going to be sharing with Joel.

"Come on, dogs. Come get a drink." Emma coaxed the dogs to the front of their room and poured them some water from the five-gallon jug they'd filled at the compound. Ben tried to discourage the dogs from drinking the rainwater as much as he could and asked the kids to do the same. They had about fifteen gallons of water on hand, plus their individual bottles, so he wasn't overly concerned about running out. Not yet, anyway.

Their water wouldn't last forever with nine people and three dogs using it, but he was fairly confident there would be opportunities ahead to refill their containers. The northern route he planned on taking would lead them around the southern edge of Lake Erie. A body of water that size should have plenty of tributaries where they could replenish their water supply. It would mean a lot of hand-pumping with the water purifier, but there were others to help with that now.

Of course, there was no guarantee they would find clean water, but lack of a sure thing was nothing new and had become a part of everyday life. But it wasn't just finding water that weighed on his mind. For all they knew, Cloverdale no longer existed and had been overrun by looters and criminals. It wasn't a pleasant thought, not just for the sake of the town, but for Ben and his crew as well.

As much as he hated to admit it, he was counting on Cloverdale. He told himself he wouldn't get his hopes up, but it was too late for that. They'd have to come up with a plan B if Cloverdale had been overrun. He wished Rita and Carlos's daughter didn't live so far out of the way. That was an option, but not one he'd given much thought to. Again, the main problem was that there was no way of knowing if their daughter's place had survived. Driving so far out of their way was too big of a risk, and it could end up costing them a couple days of travel.

Ben watched as Sandy filled her water bottle from the five-gallon jug and headed for the bathroom with the battery-powered lantern. The storm was still raging outside, and although it should have been light out, it looked much later than it actually was.

She smiled. "Should I say goodnight now? You look like you could fall asleep sitting up."

"No, I'll be here when you get out. I want to clean up a little, too, before I lie down."

"Do you want to go first? I can wait."

"You go ahead. I want to check in on the others one more time."

"Okay. I won't be long." Sandy flicked on the lantern and closed the bathroom door. Even though the room windows faced away from the road, they still needed to be careful. The curtains would block the light, but only if everyone was mindful to keep them closed. And Ben intended on making sure they all did just that. He willed himself up from his seat on the edge of the bed with the promise of returning soon.

He poked his head into the kids' room first. "Just checking to make sure your curtains are closed." They were.

The kids barely paid him any mind and continued with their conversation about the moonshiners' camp. The dogs were the only ones that gave him any attention, but they went back to napping after a few seconds. Ben was actually glad to hear the kids talking about the ordeal. It meant they were coping with what happened. That was a healthy and welcome alternative to no one ever speaking a word about it again, and it made Ben smile as he left the room. The kids were going to come out of this all right and end up as stronger individuals because of it.

Ben made his way onto the covered vestibule that ran past the other rooms. The rain had slacked off a little bit, and he was relieved to see the water level in the parking lot hadn't risen any more since they arrived. He wasn't overly concerned about being caught in a flash flood, but with their luck on this trip, he wasn't leaving anything to chance.

As tired as he was, if it kept raining like this, he'd be up at some point in the middle of the night to check the water level again. He drew in a deep breath of fresh air and blew it out loudly. The rain wasn't without benefit. The temperature had dropped significantly in the last hour or so and the air felt cleaner than it ever had. He passed Rita and Carlos's room and knocked on Martin's door.

Maybe this was just what everything needed: a good rain to wash away the ash and dust that had accumulated over the last couple of weeks.

A grayish-brown blanket of fine particles covered nearly everything. In fact, over the last week or so, in an effort to keep his hands clean, Ben had developed a habit of avoiding contact with surfaces whenever he could. The tactic had only proven mildly successful, though, and most days he gave up. It certainly hadn't been a concern over the last twenty-four hours, but he was reminded of it now as he stared at the thin film of ash on the door to Martin's room.

Ben listened carefully but didn't hear any sound. Maybe Martin was already sleeping. If that was the case, Ben wouldn't bother to wake him. He only wanted to remind him to keep his curtains drawn if he used a light, and from the outside, he could see that they were closed. He was about to turn and head back to his room when the door opened. Martin stood shirtless with a towel draped over his shoulders.

"I thought I heard someone knocking."

"Sorry to bother you. Just checking on everybody before I call it a night," Ben said.

"No problem. I was cleaning up a little before I hit the hay. Are we taking turns staying up tonight?"

"No. We all need the sleep. I'm counting on the dogs to let us know if anyone comes around." Ben shifted his stance and took the weight off his bad knee.

Martin looked relieved. "Okay, good. I'm so tired I'll probably be asleep before I hit the pillow. If you wanted someone to stay up, though, I was going to volunteer to go first and get it over with."

"Nope. You rest up. Tomorrow's going to be a long one. Keep your weapon handy, but I think we're in pretty good shape back here and I don't anticipate any trouble tonight. Besides, I doubt anyone will venture out in this if they don't have to." Ben started to back away from the door. He was anxious to return to his room and give his knee a break.

"That's true. I didn't even think of that. Well, I'll be ready if you need me." Martin glanced at his AR-15 leaning against the wall by the bed. The .45 pistol sat close by on the nightstand.

Ben nodded. "Good, let's hope we don't talk again till morning."

"Right." Martin started to close the door but stopped. "Hey, thanks for letting me tag along with you guys."

"No problem. Glad to have you with us, buddy. Goodnight now." Ben turned and walked away as Martin said goodnight and closed his door. Ben was genuinely glad to have the guy along with them. And not just because having him join meant they could carry more gear but because it made them stronger. Martin had proven himself in the firefight at the compound, and it was comforting to know there was someone else Ben could rely on when the chips were down. Martin might not have been the most accurate, but he stood his ground and laid down cover fire. And that was all Ben could really ask for.

He slowed down as he approached Rita and Carlos's room but decided not to stop. The curtains were closed and he didn't want to bother them. They were probably already sleeping anyway. He hoped he wasn't making a huge mistake by not posting someone on watch tonight; it was a gamble, for sure, but one he thought was worth the risk.

What choice did they have, really? They had to put some serious hours behind the wheel tomorrow if they were ever going to reach Cloverdale in a reasonable amount of time. The storm had already cut their efforts short today. And as much as he tried to convince himself it was okay and they'd make up some miles tomorrow, it bothered him that they hadn't made it farther away from the compound.

Ben looked over at the vehicles one more time before heading inside the room. He took a little extra time and surveyed their surroundings as well. He really was glad they weren't camping in this tonight. They probably would have ended up sleeping in the vehicles to stay dry. He'd done that before and knew they were lucky to have the motel at their disposal. There was no more thinking about it now. He closed the door quietly behind him in case anyone was sleeping. He was going to tell the kids to keep it down, but he didn't have to; Brad and Emma were both sleeping, and Joel and Allie weren't far behind.

Ben closed the door halfway and placed a trashcan against it to keep it there.

"It's all yours." Sandy was sitting on the bed closest to the bathroom and working on her nails with a file.

"Great." Ben didn't waste any time and grabbed a Nalgene full of water and a flashlight. Sandy was using the lantern and he didn't want to deny her the better light while she primped. As it was, they didn't have many luxuries, and there was no telling when they would spend the night in a place like this again.

Ben washed up as best as he could with water and the small bar of hand soap on the side of the sink. A shower would have been nice, but it was just as well they didn't have that option because he was too tired to take one anyway. He spent most of his time in the bathroom, cleaning the dried blood from under his fingernails and from the knife Allie had given him in the container. He watched the pink water disappear down the drain and hoped that was the last he ever saw of the moonshiners.

He toweled off and did his best to avoid looking at himself in the mirror while he brushed his teeth. He didn't need to see the bags under his eyes and the gray in his beard to know they were there. If he looked anything like he felt, it wasn't something he needed to focus on right now. He dried the knife off last and threw the dirt and blood-stained towel into the corner when he was done with it. Sandy was half asleep when he emerged from the bathroom and he did his best to cover the small flashlight with his hand.

He moved the KSG closer to the bed and placed his 9mm on the nightstand along with Allie's knife. He had intended to give it back to her earlier but wanted to clean the blood off first. He'd return it in the morning.

Ben turned to tell Sandy goodnight but wasn't surprised to find her already asleep. He turned the flashlight off and unlaced his boots in the dark, kicking them off quietly one by one. It felt good to free his feet from the confines of the rigid hiking boots and even better to lie down on the bed. He didn't bother getting under the covers; the softness of the bed and pillow was enough. It was the most comfort they'd been exposed to since leaving Jack's, and he was out cold before he could formulate another thought.

· 8 ·

The door burst open, sending splinters of wood flying across the room as one of the moonshiners kicked it in from its frame. Ben tried to reach for the KSG but couldn't get his body to cooperate with his thoughts. He felt trapped by the gaze of his assailant, and all he could do was stare back at the dark blank eyes that leered at him through the lenses of the gas mask.

Ben felt like his heart was going to explode and sat straight up in bed, drenched in a cold sweat. At first, he didn't know where he was, and it took him a few seconds to realize he'd been dreaming. He looked around the room, starting with the door, to make sure it really was a figment of his imagination. Rubbing his eyes, he let out a sigh of relief and checked to see if Sandy was still sleeping. She was. Thankfully, he hadn't disturbed her.

He checked his watch and saw that it was a little after five in the morning. There was no way he'd slept through the entire night without getting up at least once, but his watch didn't lie, and neither did the small trace of light slipping past the edge of the curtain. He'd meant to check on things at some point during the night, but with the way he felt before bed, unsurprisingly, he'd failed to do that. From the sounds of things, the others were still sleeping as well. At least the kids were.

They had all agreed as a group last night to try and get on the road no later than 6:30 or 7:00. Ben would have preferred to leave much earlier, but he was trying to be realistic, and more importantly, he didn't want to start the day off with an unobtainable goal or unrealistic schedule. Even though they didn't have to break camp or pack much gear before they could leave, he expected everything to take longer with nine people.

He was tempted to lie down again, and he started to before Gunner let out a low growl from the other room. His pulse quickened once more, and he froze in place and listened. Was the dog dreaming, or did Gunner actually hear something that piqued his interest? A few more minutes of rest would have felt nice, but he couldn't lie back down in good conscience. Just the thought of someone snooping around outside near the vehicles was enough to get his blood pumping; there would be no going back to sleep now.

Ben swung his legs over the bed and slowly rose

to his feet. The knee was still sore and a little swollen, but time off of it had done him good. A couple more pain pills this morning with his coffee and he'd be in better shape than he was yesterday. His side felt better, too, although it didn't appear that way in the mirror. The purple and red pancake-sized bruise on his torso looked much worse than it felt. What he originally thought was a broken rib seemed more likely to be just a bad contusion.

He stuck his head into the kids' room through the partially open door. Everyone was asleep, including the dogs, all except Gunner. As soon as he spotted Ben, he started to thump his tail on the carpet loudly.

"Shhh." Ben pointed at Gunner, but it only got the dog more excited, and he got up off the floor. Gunner approached with his head down and let out a couple more low growls while looking back toward the window.

"Well, come on then," Ben whispered. He moved the trash can out of the way and made room for Gunner to come into his and Sandy's room. Gunner acting this way didn't necessarily mean someone was outside. He might just have to go to the bathroom, but it was reason enough for Ben to check it out. And it was reason enough to take the KSG.

His head was still foggy, and he'd be better off with the shotgun than the pistol right now.

Hopefully he wouldn't need either. Maybe Gunner had heard Martin or one of the others. Whatever it was still had the dog's interest, and he went straight to the door, where he stood and waited for Ben to let him out.

"Hang on." Ben crept over to the window and parted the curtains enough to peek outside. The light he'd seen around the window's edge when he first woke up seemed to have suddenly disappeared. It was too dark to tell if anyone was out there or not.

He listened for a few seconds more while he tried to decide how he was going to handle this, but he didn't hear anything. Should he bother waking up Joel? Gunner was growing impatient and shifted his weight back and forth between his front paws while whining softly. It was way too early to be doing this. *So much for that coffee.*

Ben unlocked the deadbolt and slid the door chain out of the way, careful not to let it drop onto the door and make any noise. He turned the knob just enough to free the latch but held his foot against the door so Gunner couldn't force his snoot through the gap and open the door before he was ready. Only then did Ben realize he was barefoot, but he was already committed at this point.

With one hand on Gunner's collar and the other holding the shotgun, he eased his foot away and let the door swing open on its own. As soon as the gap was large enough, Gunner pushed his nose through and sniffed loudly at the damp morning air. Ben anticipated this and held the collar firm while staying focused on the parking lot. He searched around the vehicles but didn't notice anything out of place.

Gunner seemed a little calmer now that he'd satisfied his urge to sample the air and see outside the door for himself, and Ben felt comfortable letting go of his collar. Gunner took the liberty of moving out onto the vestibule and headed down the steps to the trucks.

"Gunner," Ben said quietly but firmly enough to make the dog stop and look back. "Easy, boy." Gunner resumed travel toward the parking lot, but at a slower pace.

The damp concrete felt cool on his bare feet, and for the first time since they'd started this journey, he would go so far as to say it felt nice outside. Although it was no longer raining, water dripped from the vestibule overhang and splashed onto the steps. The parking lot was still flooded with what Benn guessed to be at least six inches of water, judging by how high it came up on the Blazer's tire. Gunner paid it no mind, though, and waded through without a second's hesitation.

If there was anyone out here, he would have heard them moving; it would be impossible to sneak around in all this water. Maybe Gunner had been dreaming.

All the same, Ben resisted the urge to shine his flashlight on the dog just yet. Slowly, he moved along the row of vehicles, checking between each one as he made his way down the vestibule and past the doors to Rita and Carlos's room and then Martin's. He kept the KSG at the ready, but nobody was there. He relaxed when he was in line with the far side of the Scout and had Gunner in his sight once more.

The dog splashed his way through the water and rejoined Ben up on the covered walkway. Long strings of saliva and water hung from Gunner's mouth; he'd obviously been drinking from the pooled water as he waded around the vehicles. It wasn't ideal, and Ben hoped the worst of the pollutants had been washed away in the first few hours of the downpour. The water that remained was probably clean enough for the dogs to drink without suffering any consequences.

Gunner shook off and a spray of cold water landed on Ben's feet.

"Gunner." Ben shook his head. They'd have to keep the dogs out of the water before they left. Wet dogs didn't make for ideal travel companions, and even Emma, lover of all four-legged things, had her limits. He needed everyone to be as comfortable as possible today so they could make the most of their time on the road.

Ben made his way to the room, only looking

back out toward the parking lot a couple of times before sneaking back into his and Sandy's room. He was glad to see she was still sleeping. They all needed the rest, and there was no point in getting up any sooner than necessary. Besides, he enjoyed this quiet time alone in the morning; it was the only time of day when he didn't feel responsible for everyone else, at least not directly or in a way that required his immediate attention.

Ben heard Gunner. He was back in the kids' room, snorting loudly and rolling around on the carpet after his romp through the water outside. The morning quiet wouldn't last much longer, and he knew it. Once the other dogs were awake, the process would begin, and the others would follow. Ben quickened his pace with the coffee, brewing as much as possible without making too much noise himself.

Gunner returned to Ben and Sandy's room, clearly disappointed he couldn't get anyone to join in his morning festivities. Ben was only glad Gunner's grumbles hadn't materialized into a threat. Staying here at the motel turned out to be a good decision after all. They would have had a miserable night camping in the rain, and just the thought of having to pack up wet gear was enough to make him thankful they had spent the night here instead.

Ben set up the stove and coffee pot on the front table near the window. Pulling one of the padded chairs over, he took a seat.

"Gunner, come here, boy," Ben whispered. He was willing to do whatever it took to keep things calm and quiet for a little while longer, even if that meant rubbing a wet dog. Gunner didn't waste any time, pressing his snoot into Ben's leg and waiting to be scratched.

"Good boy. We just need to be quiet for a little longer. Everybody needs their sleep." Ben spoke quietly as he kept one eye on the coffee pot. Gunner wagged his tail and stared at Ben with big brown eyes, as though he understood every word. Sometimes Ben wondered if the dog was smarter than he gave him credit for. Gunner had certainly been an asset on this trip so far.

Ben saw that the coffee was ready and turned off the stove. He poured a cup and watched the steam rise as he inhaled the aroma deeply. The first sip was always the best, and he savored it, along with the quiet of the morning. He checked his watch and saw that it was approaching six. He'd give himself a little more time. Then he'd have to start waking people up. But he wouldn't think about that for now.

Ben kicked his feet up on the table and did his best not to think at all for a few minutes. Gunner looked equally content, his eyes half closed as Ben rubbed a favorite spot behind his ear. It was going to be a long day; they might as well relax for a few more minutes.

· 9 ·

Ben went through the first cup of coffee quickly and poured himself another right away. He made it halfway through the second cup when Sandy started to wake up.

"Morning." Ben parted the curtain a few inches to allow some of the morning light to penetrate the darkness of the room. The sun had barely crested the horizon, but even a little bit of light made a big difference. It was nice to see clear skies, but he couldn't help but wonder if that would translate to higher temperatures later in the day.

"Good morning." Sandy stretched and pulled herself up until she was sitting with her back against the pillows.

"Cup of coffee?" Ben asked.

"Yes, thank you."

He poured Sandy a cup and brought it over to her in bed.

"Oh, I need this so much." Sandy grasped the mug with both hands and took a drink. "That really hits the spot."

"How'd you sleep?" Ben headed back over to the window and opened the other side of the curtain as well.

"It was wonderful. Can't believe I slept all the way through the night." She rolled her eyes. "Well, actually, I can. I was exhausted. I don't even remember falling asleep."

"I know. Same here."

"Just give me a couple minutes and I'll be ready to help you with breakfast or whatever needs doing so we can get out of here." Sandy swung her legs out from under the covers. Slowly getting to her feet, she stumbled to the bathroom, coffee in hand. Since he was up, Ben peeked in on the kids one more time, but there was still no movement from their room. He checked his watch and decided to give them a few more minutes.

He'd start with the others first. Gunner followed closely as he opened the door and headed back outside. This time, Ben left the door open behind him to let some fresh air into the room. The cool concrete felt good on his feet now, unlike earlier. He could already tell that the temperature had risen slightly since he was first outside this morning. And he wondered again if clearer skies meant higher temperatures.

He didn't make it far before the still of the morning was interrupted by the sound of paws and toenails scurrying on the concrete behind him. The other two dogs were up now, too, and more than happy to follow Gunner back into the water surrounding the vehicles. *So much for keeping the dogs dry.*

As Ben watched the dogs play in the water, he wondered if they should all leave their shoes off until after the trucks were packed and they were ready to pull out. There was nothing worse than starting the day with wet boots. They'd just have to be careful and try not to step on anything sharp.

The water didn't look especially dirty, but walking around in it with an open cut would be asking for an infection. The only other option—and he didn't like it—was finding the storm drain and unclogging it. The parking lot would probably empty in minutes, but he really didn't want to take the time to fool with that right now.

Ben was about to call the dogs back up to the motel when the door to the kids' room casually swung open. It was Emma of all people, the one Ben expected to sleep the longest.

He smiled. "Good morning, sunshine."

"Morning." Emma yawned a much less enthusiastic greeting while shielding her eyes from the sun and watching the dogs race around the trucks in a game of chase. "What a mess."

"I know. Can you imagine camping in this?" Ben hoped she realized it could have been much worse.

"I don't even want to think about it." She yawned again.

"So you think you can get them under control while I check on our friends?" Ben asked.

"Yeah," Emma mumbled, still not yet fully awake.

"Are the others up?"

"Just Joel and Allie. Brad is still sleeping." Emma rubbed her eyes and barely moved out of the way in time to avoid the train of dogs that flew by her. They'd spotted her from the parking lot, and the excitement had sent them into another wild burst of energy that included a full-speed run past her and Ben and down the length of the vestibule.

"Well, don't let your brother sleep too long. We're going to get breakfast started soon so we can get back on the road." Ben turned to walk away but stopped. "And try to keep those dogs dry, okay?"

"I'll try." Emma shuffled to the edge of the concrete and clapped her hands to get the dogs' attention. Ben didn't mind them blowing off a little steam, but he was still concerned about the amount of noise they were making. Things had gone well for them here, and he didn't want to let his guard down when they were this close to leaving. Now was the time to play it safe, and that meant not drawing any unwanted attention.

Ben decided to take a stroll to the end of the covered walkway, where he would have a view of the main road that ran past the motel and out to the highway. Unfortunately, he still had the KSG. If he'd thought this through better, he would have brought his rifle with the scope. But for now, all he really wanted to do was confirm they were still alone.

He stopped just shy of the corner and slowly looked around to the road beyond the parking lot. It was bright enough outside that he could see the street was empty and absent of any movement. Satisfied all was still quiet, he headed for Martin's room. He was hoping to find him awake but wouldn't be surprised if he wasn't.

Ben rapped his knuckles on the door quietly at first, then a little louder after a couple of seconds went by. When Martin finally answered the door, he looked rough and Ben figured he must have been sleeping.

"Hope you got some sleep. We've got a big drive ahead of us today." Ben glanced out at the trucks.

Martin passed a hand through his disheveled hair. "I did pretty well. Only woke up once or twice. After a little breakfast, I'll be ready to hit the road."

"I've got some coffee going in our room. Come on down and grab some when you're ready," Ben offered.

"Thanks, I appreciate that. Are we just doing MREs on our own this morning?" Martin asked.

"Yeah, I think that's best. It'll be quick, at least, and get us back on the road sooner. I'm hoping to put this state behind us today and at least be within a couple hours of the separation point with Rita and her husband, if all goes well."

"Where will that be?"

"I was thinking somewhere north of Columbus. That's the closest we'll come to Fort Wayne before heading west again toward Indianapolis."

"You think they'll be okay on their own?" Martin raised his brow.

"I think they'll be fine, but we'll see how the day goes. I won't let them get in over their heads," Ben assured him.

"It took all they had yesterday to keep up with us," Martin added.

"Today is a new day. Let's hope a good night's sleep has done them some good." Ben headed toward the couple's room as they spoke. "I'll see you down at the room for some coffee."

"All right. I'll be down in a few." Martin closed his door.

Been kept the conversation about Rita and Carlos generic. But the fact was, he'd given the situation a lot of thought. He knew the exact location on the map where they would part ways. He also knew the older couple might not be able to finish the trip on their own, and ignoring that fact wouldn't make the problem go away. Martin mentioning it only served to remind him of the possibility. A scenario that involved the whole convoy escorting Rita and Carlos to their daughter's house in Fort Wayne might be unavoidable.

Ben paused for a moment, then knocked on the older couple's door. Before talking to them, he wanted to clear his mind of any preconceived notions about their ability to keep up with the travel routine today. It was too early, and he didn't want to start the day with negative thoughts. Besides, it wasn't their fault they'd been held hostage for two weeks and given inadequate food and water. He didn't know their daughter, but he was certain she would want him and the others to do everything in their power to make sure her parents made it to Fort Wayne.

Rita opened the door quickly and caught him off guard. "Good morning, Ben."

"Morning." Ben nodded. "How did you all sleep last night?"

"Oh, it was wonderful. It's been a while since we've been that comfortable. Not even Carlos's snoring could keep me up." She smiled.

"Glad to hear it. I just wanted to check in with you guys and let you know that we're gonna try and get out of here in the next half hour or so. We're all just going to eat MREs on our own this morning and make it a quick breakfast."

"We've already eaten. Just enjoying our coffee now."

"Hey there, Ben," Carlos said but stayed seated at the small table by the door.

Ben waved. "Hey, good morning. Let me know when you've got your things packed and one of us will help you get it loaded into the truck. It's still pretty deep out there and I don't want you getting all wet." Ben looked over his shoulder at the Toyota pickup sitting in the massive puddle that used to be a parking lot.

Rita nodded. "Oh my, that looks deep."

"I'm sure the storm drains are filled with trash, but we'll help get you out of here dry," Ben added.

"Thank you." Rita smiled and placed a hand on Ben's arm. "How are you feeling today?"

"Better, thanks." He rubbed his hand across his ribs. He did feel better now, even better than when he first woke up. Of course, the pain medicine he downed with the first cup of coffee had more to do with how he felt than anything else.

"You take care of yourself and let Sandy drive some today. Those kids need you good and healthy," she said sternly.

"Yes, ma'am." Ben smiled and began to leave.

"We'll be packed up and ready to leave whenever you say." Rita left the door ajar as she returned to the table to join her husband.

Something about Rita's voice made him not want to disappoint her. And she was right; his body still needed time to heal. But he'd never been one to sit around idly while others participated. He'd let Sandy do her share of the driving today, but there were four vehicles now, and the possibility of filling in for another driver was likely and not something he would shy away from if need be.

At least Rita's responses this morning were promising. She seemed much more energetic than yesterday, and Ben hoped her husband looked and felt the same. He was encouraged by the encounter with them and had high hopes for the day. And at this point, he was more concerned about Martin than the old couple, although Martin would probably be fine after he got a little coffee in him and had a chance to fully wake up.

When Ben entered his room, Sandy was out of the bathroom and working on breakfast. She had a fresh pot of coffee brewing and what looked like a good start on packing her bag.

"I got the kids moving, finally. They're getting cleaned up and making breakfast for themselves," she said.

"Good." Ben was expecting more resistance from everyone this morning, but it wasn't going that way at all. He'd underestimated their desire and their understanding about needing to move on from here. As comfortable as the motel was, and as nice as it was to have a real bed last night, none of them could question the importance of leaving before they wore out their welcome. Everything was running smoothly so far, and that was what worried him the most.

· 10 ·

Three loud knocks on the door in rapid succession startled Ben, but not as much as it did Sandy. Ben was expecting Martin to come to their room for coffee, and now he regretted not telling him to just come on in when he was ready.

"Who's that?" Sandy said.

"It's probably Martin. I told him to come get some coffee earlier." Ben started for the door, but before he could reach it, Martin burst into the room. His face was flush; he must have run full tilt to their room.

"People… There's people out there!" While Martin caught his breath, Ben and Sandy stared at each other for a few seconds in total silence before the gravity of the situation sank in. Ben's worst fears about staying here had been realized. He felt the full effects of the coffee now, coupled with a surge of adrenaline coursing through his veins.

His mind began to race, but before he assumed the worst, he needed to investigate for himself.

Ben opted for the M24 this time and snatched the 9mm off the nightstand for good measure.

"What do we do?" Sandy's relaxed demeanor and friendly smile were gone now.

"Martin and I will check it out. Tell Joel and the other kids what's going on and have them help you get things packed up and into the trucks. We may need to make a hasty exit." Ben tucked his pistol and concealed carry holster into his waistband, then pulled his shirt down over it.

"There must... There must be a few of them. I can hear them talking," Martin stammered. That wasn't what Ben wanted to hear.

"Better yet, get the bags ready but don't load the trucks yet. I want everybody to stay in their rooms for now, at least until I figure out what's going on." Ben didn't want to jump the gun on this and ruin their morning. Maybe it was just a couple of harmless travelers walking by on the road. But his gut and their experiences so far told him that probably wasn't the case. *So much for a relaxing start to the day.*

Ben looked at Martin. "Come on, let's go."

He poked his head in the kids' door on the way by and told them Sandy would explain everything and that they were to keep their door closed until he returned. Ben stopped at the next room down and briefly let Rita and Carlos know what was going on. He wished he had taken the time to cover the vehicles with the camouflage netting last night. He thought about it too late and couldn't muster the energy to get out of bed and do it, a mistake he hoped they all didn't live to regret.

He was trying to listen for voices, but as they made their way down the vestibule, all he could hear was Martin's heavy breathing behind him. He was going to have to calm the guy down somehow or he wasn't going to be much help. In hindsight, Ben should have left Martin to help with the packing and taken Joel instead.

Ben stopped at the corner of the building and crouched down. He looked back at Martin. "Okay, we can take it easy for a minute." He didn't want the guy passing out on him. Martin nodded and stared down at the ground as he inhaled deeply. Ben wondered if he was having some kind of panic attack. He hadn't even gotten this worked up during the gunfight at the compound.

Martin's breathing quieted eventually, and Ben was able to hear distant voices. How Martin had heard them initially was a mystery; he must have been outside by the trucks. It sounded like a man and a woman arguing and reminded him of a TV show playing in the background. He unslung his M24 and scoped the street from one end to the other but saw nothing.

Ben gave the street another pass with his scope, slower this time, pausing at some of the smashed-out storefronts along the way. His patience paid off and he spotted something. There was someone inside the remains of a drugstore on the corner. By the looks of it, the old concrete building had been plundered long ago, and only a few badly cracked windows remained. He could see shadows moving behind the filthy glass.

"The drugstore, on the corner," Ben said softly, even though the looters couldn't have heard him from this distance. They must have been outside on the street when Martin heard them before. They were likely going from store to store, looking for any supplies that might have been missed by the initial mob of looters. *Good luck with that.* All the places Ben had stopped to fuel up had been picked clean. The one convenience store where the kids lucked out and found a case of water hidden under the shelves was the only exception.

"How many are there?" Martin asked.

"I can't tell yet. They're inside the store." Ben wondered if this was what Gunner had heard early this morning. That made no difference now, although he vowed to investigate Gunner's premonitions more thoroughly from this point forward. He was relieved that the looters hadn't spotted their vehicles, at least not yet.

"I don't think they know we're here. I'd say

we're okay for the time being. No need to get too excited yet. But we need to keep an eye on them." Ben wasn't overly concerned about the looters' presence. Maybe that was because of what they had just gone through with the moonshiners. He was more irritated than worried. He felt a sense of defiance about the situation. They deserved to be here as much as the looters did. And the thought of rushing everyone out of here under duress irritated him even more; these people had interrupted his otherwise peaceful morning.

"Do you want me to go back and tell everybody to get ready to leave?" Martin sounded better now, his breathing close to normal.

"Tell the others to continue getting their stuff together. It's okay to pack the trucks, but no slamming doors. And tell them to finish eating breakfast. I think we'll just wait the looters out. There can't be anything left of any value. I'm hoping they'll give up and be on their way soon." Ben looked away from his scope and caught Martin as he was about to leave. "Hey, can you bring back one of the radios?"

"Sure." And with that, Martin was gone. He was a good guy. A little excitable, but solid so far when it came to taking orders. Martin did best when given specific jobs, even if it did require a little extra instruction at times. It was nice to take some of the burden off Joel, and Ben liked being able to leave his oldest with the younger two, especially in situations like this. It wasn't that he didn't trust Sandy or Allie to look out for the kids, but Joel felt a special responsibility for his brother and sister, and that made him a good babysitter by default.

Ben kept the scope trained on the storefront. Hopefully Martin wouldn't take too long getting back to him with the radio. He wanted to be in direct communication with the others in case the situation changed, something that was no longer only a concern these days but more like an expectation. Suddenly, Ben saw a flurry of movement, and a split second later, a small display case came flying through the window, shattering it into hundreds of pieces. Large shards of glass landed on the sidewalk in front of the store. The display landed on its side and skidded to a stop in the street, leaving behind a trail of parts.

Ben watched intently as the scene unfolded. The looters inside the building were now in plain sight thanks to the missing window. The way these people were dressed made him think of the moonshiners immediately. But maybe he thought that only because in the back of his mind, he half expected them to show up here this morning.

The small group inside the drugstore comprised two men and a woman. And the men looked to be in the middle of a heated argument, which explained the display case being launched through the window. One had the other backed up against the opening while the woman watched in the background. She didn't seem overly concerned with the scuffle, though; she continued looking around the place for anything of value. Her movements weren't smooth but erratic, and occasionally, she appeared to shout at no one in particular.

At first, Ben thought they were drunk; he knew firsthand that moonshine was in ready supply around these parts. But as he observed their actions and mannerisms from a distance, he began to think it was something else. If he had to guess, he would say they were high on something. He would have preferred drunks over whatever these people were. By the looks of things, he guessed that whatever they were on was in full effect.

Ben remembered an incident that happened not too far from his store in Durango. A guy on meth wandered into one of the local coffee shops and started tearing the place apart. It was only a few doors down from the store, so Ben ran outside to see what was going on when he heard the commotion. He was just in time to see three cops wrestling with a guy on the ground. It took all the officers had to subdue the man and stuff him into the back of the patrol car.

He'd watched them drive away with the man in custody, kicking the safety divider with his bare feet and screaming at the top of his lungs—but only after he'd exhausted his efforts to smash the rear window with his head.

One of the officers stayed behind to talk to the nearby business owners about what had happened, and Ben had a chance to ask a few questions of his own. As it turned out, it wasn't their first run-in with the guy. He was a known meth user they'd had plenty of problems with in the past. Ben was by far no expert, but he'd venture to guess that was exactly what these people were on.

Their best bet to avoid trouble with the druggies was to stay off their radar. With any luck, they'd lose interest soon and go away. Meanwhile, Ben and his crew could stay here and finish their breakfast while they waited. They'd have to keep an eye on the meth heads as long as they stayed at the motel. It was a mitigated risk, one he'd gladly accept over a gang of moonshiners looking for revenge.

· 11 ·

Martin finally returned with the radio and a small bag thrown over his shoulder. He crouched down next to Ben and leaned his AR-15 against the brick wall of the motel.

"Here you go. Brought you something to eat." Martin pulled an MRE out of the backpack and handed it to Ben, then reached back into the bag and retrieved a pair of binoculars.

"Thanks." Ben held up the MRE. "You know there's an SKS in the back of the Scout with a nice optic on it. It's a little cumbersome, but I could teach you how to operate it and you'd have something better-equipped for a long-range shot." Ben eyeballed Martin's open-sighted rifle.

"Yeah, I'd like that," Martin answered.

"Good, we'll do that when we get a chance. Hey, do you mind keeping an eye on those guys while I eat?" Ben noticed Martin was busy watching the action at the drugstore.

"Yeah, no problem. Take your time." Martin spoke without looking down from the binoculars. Ben tore into the bag and got started preparing the main meal pouch before he realized he didn't have the radio.

"Did you remember the radio?" Ben searched the ground, thinking maybe Martin had set it by his rifle and he hadn't noticed.

"Oh yeah, sorry. Here it is." Martin reached back into the bag and pulled out the small two-way. "Joel's got the other one."

"Thanks." Ben didn't waste any time switching on the radio while he tore open a small pouch of peanut butter with his teeth.

"Come in, Joel. Over."

"Joel here. What's going on? Over."

"Just some looters out on Main Street. I'll eat my breakfast here and keep an eye on them. You guys keep packing up and let me know when you're ready to roll out. Over." Ben tried to sound casual; he didn't want Joel or the other kids to worry.

That was the whole purpose of waiting the druggies out: not causing a scene or creating a situation that required force to get out of. He just wanted them all to have a low-key morning, especially after what they'd been through over the last couple of days. If that meant waiting at the motel for an extra half hour, so be it.

"Putting on quite the show, aren't they?" Martin was still watching the looters through the binoculars.

"Yeah, they're a mess, all right." Ben was too hungry to look away from his meal.

"I've seen people acting like that around the Hill District in Pittsburgh. It's a bad section of..." Martin paused for a moment and looked away from the binoculars before returning his attention to the looters. "It *was* a bad section of the city. I had to drive through it every day on my way to and from work."

"Oh, they're on something, all right. There's no doubt about it," Ben huffed.

"There was a time when my wife and I thought nothing of running into the city for a meal. But that changed a long time ago. Pittsburgh went downhill fast over the last few years. I've seen it with my own eyes. I won't even stop for gas in some areas anymore. The meth and opioid addicts have taken over the run-down neighborhoods." Martin put the binoculars down and shook his head. "We were gonna move away when I retired."

Ben thought about Martin's story and wondered how many places across the country it could have been applied to. A lot, he was willing to bet. Even Durango was no longer a place Ben considered immune to these things, either. He'd watched the town undergo some big changes since he was a kid, and part of him was glad his parents weren't around to see what had become of their once sleepy little mountain town. Durango's saving grace was its location; he could drive out of town and be in the middle of nowhere within minutes. That and the fact that he lived above it all—literally, at nine thousand feet.

"Pittsburgh wasn't the only place with problems." Ben glanced at Martin between bites of food.

"Things were getting pretty bad before all this, weren't they?" Martin shifted his weight to the other knee.

"They were." Ben swallowed the last bite of his MRE and began stuffing his trash into the main pouch.

"Um, you mind if I head back to my room? I didn't get a chance to, ah, finish cleaning up this morning. There are still some things I'd like to take care of, if you know what I mean. Just because there's no water doesn't mean I can't use the toilet once, although I might not get the room deposit back with the way my stomach feels." Martin made a face while rubbing his belly and laughing about it.

Ben held up his hand. "Go ahead. I got it." He didn't need to hear any more about Martin's morning plans. He thought about telling him the toilet could be flushed by dumping water into the bowl, but that would be a waste of resources they might regret later. Besides, it really didn't matter how they left this place.

"Thanks. Let Joel know if you need anything. I'll be happy to run it out to you." Martin almost left his rifle but stopped to grab it before heading for his room. Ben had to laugh a little bit. Joking around was Martin's way of dealing with tough situations. It was better than the alternative of being down and gloomy, even if at times his sense of humor was a bit childish. There were plenty of reasons for Martin to have a bad attitude; he'd been dealt some pretty tough cards. A lesser man would have called it quits long before now. And Ben thought it was a testament to the guy's character, the way he carried on in spite of things.

Ben thought about something Martin had said before he hurried off: *Things were getting pretty bad before all this, weren't they?* He was right about that. Long before the EMPs hit, the country was going downhill fast. At least it seemed that way on TV. The riots and protests were far from peaceful, and violent acts replaced words.

This wasn't the first time Ben thought about it, how in some small way, what was happening right now wasn't all bad. And although the staggering amount of life lost was a terrible thing, he wondered if all this was inevitable sooner or later.

If it wasn't for the EMPs, he thought the country was headed for some type of civil war in his lifetime.

The nation was too divided. No one trusted politicians or the government anymore. The media seemed intent on pushing a divisive agenda. And overall, Ben thought the country as a whole had lost its moral compass long ago. Foreign money had infected the system to the point where there were no longer repercussions for breaking the law if you were rich enough or powerful enough. Law and order had lost all meaning to the wealthy elite.

The current worldview of the United States was not a good one. And Ben wondered if any of their supposed allies would come to their aid. If they did, he was sure help wouldn't come without a price. He thought most other countries would likely watch from afar, at least for a while, or until the threat of radiation poisoning subsided. Outside of not getting involved in a nuclear war, there were other reasons for countries to keep their distance. One of the biggest was that the U.S. didn't have anything to offer them in return anymore. It was a harsh reality, but one he thought was true.

He was scared for the children's future, but there was nothing he could do about it. Teaching them how to survive in a post-apocalyptic world was the best he could offer them. He hoped it was enough.

He didn't just want them to survive, though. He wanted them to live fulfilling lives and have families of their own. That all seemed like a lot to hope for, given the current situation, and he just wasn't sure if that was possible anymore.

Ben took up his M24 and looked through the scope to see what the looters were up to now. His heart skipped a beat when he saw an empty drugstore. Then he realized they'd moved to the next building down the road in the direction of the motel. He had no reason to be concerned yet; they were still a good distance away.

All right, any day now. Wrap it up. Ben wondered how long they'd have to wait this out and began thinking of other ways out of here. Or he could just say screw it, get the trucks loaded, and leave whenever they pleased. What would the looters do about it? They might make a small scene or throw something as the trucks drove past.

The kids had certainly seen worse. But there was more to consider with four vehicles. What the first vehicle avoided, the last vehicle in the convoy would have to deal with. And his biggest concern was if the looters were armed; he couldn't tell from this distance. Then another thought came to mind. What if they had a vehicle and decided to chase after the trucks as they left?

He knew one thing for sure: all this waiting was making him anxious, and he'd grown tired of watching their drug-fueled antics a while ago. Ben's mind started to drift to a darker place, and he began having thoughts he would have been embarrassed to admit in front of his children—or any of the others, for that matter. He could easily take out all three looters right from where he was sitting, and they could drive out of town at their leisure, with a zero percent chance of an incident.

Ben pulled away from the scope and looked off toward the horizon. He inhaled deeply and released the air slowly, keeping his eyes closed. If the kids ever found out he shot and killed three unarmed people who didn't pose an immediate threat, he would never be able to look them in the eye again. He couldn't do it; he wasn't a murderer. He had enough blood on his hands already. These looter meth heads would get more grace today than they likely deserved.

Ben was startled from his thoughts by the sound of a dog barking. He turned toward the trucks and, to his disappointment, saw all three dogs come flying out of the room, one after another. All of them began running hysterically around the vehicles, barking and growling as they went. They were chasing something and splashing water several feet into the air while doing so. So much for flying below the radar on this one.

· 12 ·

"Stop! Get back here!" Emma was the first one out of the room. Stopping at the edge of the concrete walkway, she called after the dogs much louder than she should have, although Ben doubted her voice could be heard over the ruckus the dogs were making. He scrambled to his feet and ran as fast as he could back toward the rooms. Joel and the others, except for Martin, were outside on the vestibule by the time he got there. Sandy looked as confused as he was.

"Hey, what's going on here?" Ben glanced at the kids, but only for a moment, before turning his attention to the parking lot and the dogs. "Get back here. Right now. Gunner. Come here now," he shouted louder than he wanted to, but he was cutting his losses. It was either that or continue letting the dogs carry on and draw attention to themselves.

"There was a rat in the room. The dogs started

freaking out, so I opened the door to try and let it escape. We couldn't stop the dogs from following. It's my fault." Joel ran after the dogs, into the water, and Emma followed him. Bajer was the first to surrender, tail between her legs and showing clear remorse for her actions. Gunner and Sam were less ashamed of their lack of self-control and returned as though they had just gone for a romp around the yard. Gunner even stopped for a drink in the nearly belly-high water before conceding defeat and joining the other dogs on dry ground.

"Get them inside...please." Ben struggled to control his frustration.

"Sorry." Emma looked down at the ground.

"It's okay. It's not your fault. It's no one's fault. Things happen. Just get the dogs back inside for now, please, and try to get them cleaned up as much as you can." Ben's voice got softer as he spoke; he realized the kids hadn't meant any harm and the dogs were just being dogs. That didn't help alleviate his concerns that they'd been heard by the looters, though. "How 'bout everybody brings their stuff out onto the sidewalk and gets it ready to go into the trucks? I'm gonna go check on the looters and see if they heard the commotion. I'll be right back."

Ben didn't wait for an answer. Instead, he turned and headed back to the corner of the building. Maybe they'd get lucky and the ruckus would go unnoticed. Maybe the looters were so high they wouldn't care. Ben didn't put much hope in either possibility.

When he reached the corner of the building, he already had his rifle up to his shoulder. He spotted the looters immediately, and to his disappointment, they were heading straight for the motel. He wasn't surprised, but a part of him was hoping they would somehow slip out of here unnoticed. Maybe the looters wouldn't be able to figure out where the sound had come from.

Ben watched for a few seconds longer as the three made their way across the street. Their progress was slow and their movements erratic, but they were definitely headed toward the motel. He figured he had a few more minutes before the looters discovered the vehicles. There might be enough time to get the trucks loaded and drive out of here before they were forced into a confrontation with the meth-fueled bunch, but it wasn't looking good.

Ben lowered his rifle and shook his head; this wasn't how he wanted to leave here today. They'd been so careful to stay out of sight and avoid drawing any attention to themselves. It was all for nothing now. The feeling of having to constantly be on the move to stay safe was becoming commonplace, and he didn't like it one bit.

Ben watched the three strangers approach for a few moments more without the use of the scope while he accepted the inevitable. A new day, another encounter. He preferred the period right after the EMPs hit, when everyone was in hiding. Slinging the rifle over his shoulder, he headed back to the others at a quick pace. A collection of bags was already piled up outside the rooms and Joel was working on moving them to the appropriate vehicles with Allie's help.

Glad he hadn't put on his shoes yet, he set his rifle down so he could help Joel and Allie move the rest of the bags quickly. The water was up to his shins and felt disgustingly warm as he waded through it. He was careful to watch where he stepped as much as possible, although it was difficult in the brown, murky water.

"They heard all that. I figure we only have a couple minutes until they're here. I'm not overly concerned, but I'd rather avoid them if possible." Ben hoisted a bag onto his shoulder.

"Are they bad people?" Brad asked.

"They could be." Ben didn't want to get anyone overly worried, but he didn't want to downplay the threat too much. He also wanted them to keep moving quickly.

"I got the dogs as clean as I could, but they're just going to get wet again getting into the trucks." Emma emerged from the kids' room, preventing the dogs from squeezing through the door as she joined the others outside.

"Yeah, I know. We'll just have to do the best we can." Ben nodded. Spending the day in the truck with wet, smelly dogs wouldn't be any fun, but they had bigger things to worry about right now.

"When do you want me to try to load them up?" Emma asked.

"Might as well get them in now," Ben said.

"I'll help you, Em." Sandy came out of the room, her arms filled with bags and gear. "I think this is all of it except for a few small things."

Ben didn't realize they'd brought so much stuff inside with them last night. Sandy walked to the edge of the concrete and handed off her things to Ben.

"Has anyone seen Martin?" Ben hadn't noticed him helping.

"Not since he came back and went into his room," Allie answered. Ben wished Martin would hurry up. At the moment, he was proving to be their weakest link. Even Rita and Carlos were chipping in with the packing.

Bang, bang, bang. Ben pounded on Martin's door with the side of his fist. "Hey, Martin. We need to get going. Now." Ben didn't wait more than a couple of seconds before opening the door on his own and looking inside the room.

"I'll be out in a sec," Martin yelled from the bathroom.

"They're headed our way. We need to move out ASAP," Ben shouted back before slamming the door closed once more. There was no time for conversation right now. He couldn't do anything about Martin's speed, but he could grab the remaining items from his and Sandy's room and load them into the Blazer while they waited.

Sandy and Emma already had Sam in the Blazer, and Ben was pleased to see Rita and Carlos sitting in the Toyota, ready to go. He never would have guessed the older couple would be the first ones ready this morning. Of course, they had plenty of help from Joel and Allie. Brad was in the back of the Jeep while Allie handed him gear through the rolled-up side panel. Joel nearly ran into Ben coming out of the kids' room with Gunner in his arms.

"Look out. Coming through," Joel grunted as he carried the big dog above the water at a swift pace and dumped him in the back of the Jeep with Brad. Gunner looked indignant about the whole process but at least remained dry.

"Stay." Joel looked Gunner in the eye until the dog sat down with a grumble. Sandy and Emma used the same tactic with Bajer and managed to get the smaller dog loaded into the Blazer with Sam. Ben wanted to do a final sweep of his and Sandy's room to make sure they hadn't left anything behind.

"Here, would you put this in the truck for me?" Ben handed Sandy his M24. "Everybody check your rooms and make sure you have everything." The first thing he grabbed was the Kel-Tec shotgun, then Allie's pocketknife, which was still sitting on the nightstand. Finally, he did a quick sweep of the room to make sure Sandy hadn't missed anything else. Satisfied they had everything, Ben headed back outside.

He took a quick look around, making sure to check in the direction he expected the looters to come from. He was tempted to run to the corner of the building again to check on their progress but decided his time would be better spent getting everyone into the vehicles and making sure they were ready to pull out. He also noticed Martin was still missing from the group. What part of ASAP did the man not understand?

Ben ran down to Martin's room and pounded on the door once more.

"I'm coming. Just grabbing my stuff," Martin called out before Ben had a chance to say anything.

"Dad." Ben knew by the tone of Joel's voice that something was wrong. When he turned to look at his son, Joel's gaze shot past him. Ben spun around to find the three meth head looters staring at them from around the corner of the building.

"Everybody get in their vehicles," Ben instructed. Keeping his eyes on the three strangers, he readied the shotgun at his side. Slowly, the looters came from around the corner and stood in the open. Up close, they looked even worse than Ben expected. Their pale skin was covered with blisters and scabs. The rips in their clothing revealed that the rest of their bodies were covered with what Ben could only assume were radiation burns. The woman and one of the men looked to have been affected the most, resulting in missing patches of hair on their heads.

They stared at Ben and the others in silence for what felt like an eternity. Their sullen faces and bloodshot eyes almost made Ben feel sorry for them until they started to advance toward the trucks.

"Come on, load up." Ben glanced back at the others and encouraged them to move into the vehicles before bringing the shotgun up to his shoulder and pointing it at the looters. Gunner let out a few low growls from the Jeep, as if to back him up.

"Don't come any closer." Ben hated everything about this situation, and judging by the look on his daughter's face, he wasn't the only one. Just the sight of these people alone was enough to give her nightmares. Between their drug-addled movements and their overall sketchy appearance, they more closely resembled extras in a zombie movie than human beings. Ben looked back to make sure the others were doing as he asked and was glad to see Emma already in the Blazer. He could see her through the side window; she was hiding as best as she could between Sam and Bajer.

He turned his attention back to the three strangers who were still approaching at an unsteady pace.

"I said stop." Ben raised his voice and spoke firmly. What in the world was taking Martin so long? They would have been on their way by now if it weren't for him. The last thing Ben wanted to do was shoot these people. Not for his sake or theirs, but for that of the kids. Not this close and in broad daylight. They would never be able to unsee the damage the shotgun would do to a body at this range. No one needed that image burned into their memories.

Two of the looters slowed their progress and finally stopped, but one of the men continued awkwardly toward them. Ben noticed the crazed look in his eye and could see his threats were having no impact on the man. He spotted a large hunting knife stuck through the meth head's belt. It was visible now as the man's shaky hand began to creep toward it, pushing his shirt aside.

Was the man desperate enough to risk his life for whatever supplies he hoped to steal? Or maybe he wanted to be put out of his misery. Judging by his looks, Ben leaned toward the latter. He should have obliged the guy by dropping him in his tracks, and he might have if the kids weren't watching. Instead, he aimed to the left a few inches and prepared to squeeze off a round into one of the windows just ahead of the advancing looter. If that didn't deter him, there would be no more warnings, kids or no kids.

· 13 ·

Boom. The shotgun blast was magnified substantially by the partially enclosed vestibule as it echoed off the brick exterior of the motel and resonated down the corridor. Ben closed his eyes immediately after he pulled the trigger, worried some of the glass or brick might blow back in his direction.

The butt of the KSG dug into his shoulder, and he knew right away there was something different about the way it felt. In that moment, he remembered the shotgun was loaded with the incendiary Dragon's Breath ammunition from Jack's. It was meant to intimidate the moonshiners in the wide-open compound, not be fired at a wall ten feet away. Ben opened his eyes partway, only to be blinded by a shower of sparks and a white-hot fireball that smashed the window into hundreds of pieces.

Dozens of magnesium fragments bounced

around under the covered walkway and melted their way through the vinyl soffit ceiling of the vestibule. Ben did his best to shield himself from the debris. He felt like he was inside the grand finale on the Fourth of July. He lowered his arm slowly and tried to catch a glimpse of the looters through the deluge of sparks.

Ben was most concerned about the guy with the knife, although he couldn't imagine the man would still be advancing toward him through all this. Suddenly, there was yelling that rapidly increased in pitch and intensity. Ben took a few steps back until he was almost in front of Martin's room. He recognized the scream to be one of agony and panic, and a few seconds later, he knew why.

From the smoke and remaining sparks, the man who had been advancing toward Ben with the knife emerged with parts of his clothing on fire. He continued screaming as he ran down the walkway toward the vehicles, and Ben prepared to shoot again. But the man dropped the knife and veered off at the last second, launching himself into the pool of standing water surrounding the trucks. He thrashed about wildly, attempting to douse the flames without much luck at first. Some larger chunks of magnesium must have lodged them-selves under his clothing—or, at that range, maybe even under his skin.

This was not what Ben wanted to happen.

In fact, quite the opposite. He'd completely forgotten about loading the KSG with those shells back at the compound. Those rounds were meant to be his Hail Mary if things had turned dire with the moonshiners. If he'd realized that ahead of time, he would have used his pistol to make a point.

He looked to see what had become of the other two looters, but they were long gone, doing their best to run back across the parking lot, toward where they had come from, tripping and falling down several times in their haste. He turned his attention back to the man in the water. His clothes were smoldering now, but it didn't matter; he was dead. At least Ben assumed he was. His limp body lay face-down in the water.

Martin's door flung open. "Jiminy crickets! What's going on out here?" His eyes were wide as he fumbled with the belt on his pants and coughed at the lingering smoke. Ben was startled by his appearance and swung the shotgun in his direction. But he quickly moved the muzzle away once he realized it was Martin.

"Where have you been?" Ben tried to control his frustration.

"I'm sorry. I tried to be as quick as I could." Martin's expression changed from surprised to embarrassed.

Ben exhaled loudly and shook his head.

"Doesn't matter. Let's just get out of here." Martin continued to apologize as he grabbed the remainder of his things and waded through the shin-deep water to the Scout. He eyeballed the body half floating in the water but didn't say anything about it, and he didn't ask any more questions about what happened with the looters.

"Come on, we need to get the trucks away from the building." Ben spoke loud enough for the others to hear, but no one moved. They were all still in shock at the events that had just unfolded right in front of them. Ben hadn't fully processed them, either; everything had all happened so fast. But there wasn't time for that now. The roof over the vestibule was starting to burn, and so was the room the fireball had landed in.

The smoke was getting thicker by the second, and he was beginning to worry it would draw more attention to his group. There was a chance the looters weren't alone.

"Are you okay?" Sandy said from the passenger seat of the Blazer. Ben was relieved to see that she was going to let him drive without giving him any grief about it. Now wasn't the time to worry about a few aches and pains anyway. Plus, he wanted to drive right now. He felt like that was at least the one thing he could control.

"Yeah, I'm fine." He looked down at his body and clothing to double-check he was actually all right.

But other than a few singed hairs on his arms, he'd survived unscathed.

Joel started the Jeep and began to back away from the motel. "That was crazy. Was that one of those Dragon's Breath shells from Grandpa's?"

"Yeah. That wasn't the plan. I forgot I had those in there," Ben lamented. He hated how the morning had played out so far. In all his efforts to give the kids a normal start to the day, he'd managed to accomplish the exact opposite. In fact, he'd set a man on fire in front of everyone, a man who was armed with nothing more than a knife and was clearly desperate. What kind of lesson was he teaching the kids now? And while he knew it really wasn't Martin's fault, at the moment, he was having a hard time not laying blame squarely on the man.

Ben climbed into the Blazer and stood on the doorsill so he could see over the roof to the other vehicles. "I'll bring up the rear until we get back out on the highway. Everybody go in the order the trucks are in now." Ben would be more comfortable if he could keep an eye on the entire group for the time being. He watched as the others nodded in agreement from their vehicles.

It would be Martin in the Scout first, then Rita and Carlos, followed by Joel, with the Blazer bringing up the rear. Ben slid down into the seat and fired up the old Chevy, breathing a small sigh of relief that the truck started without any problems. It wasn't that he expected any, but with the number of miles they were putting on the vehicles, mechanically speaking, every good day was a gift not to be taken for granted.

With all four vehicles backed out of their parking spaces, they began to wind their way through the parking lot and toward the main road. This was also the way the looters had run, and Ben kept his eyes peeled for any signs of them, although after what happened to their friend, he doubted they would still be around. He was more concerned they would run back to a larger group and alert others to their presence in town. They only needed a few minutes to make it out to the highway and put this place in their rearview mirror. He hoped they had that much time.

"Wow, that really took off fast." Sandy was staring back at the motel. Emma was watching as well. The section of the building they had stayed in was fully engulfed in flames and would soon look like the rest of the places around here. As they weaved their way through the wrecked cars that littered Main Street, Ben was careful to keep an eye out behind them while admiring the growing inferno.

Martin seemed to be driving slower than normal this morning, too slow for Ben's liking and what the situation called for. And while Ben appreciated him taking it easy on the old Scout for a change, now wasn't the time. He honked the Blazer's horn a couple of times and stuck his hand out the window, indicating for everyone to pick up the pace. Martin was probably holding back because he knew he screwed up this morning and nearly caused a lot more trouble than necessary.

Fortunately, Martin was paying attention and saw Ben waving at him from the back of the convoy. The Scout's exhaust note picked up, and pretty soon they were increasing speed. Ben had forgotten about his knee in the fray but was noticing the pain now that he was sitting still. Once they put this place behind them, he'd be more than happy to let Sandy take over behind the wheel for a while.

As they drove by, Ben glanced over at the gas station where they fueled up last night.

"That sure was a crazy storm last night." Sandy was looking over at the gas station as well.

"It was nice to get the rain, but we could have done without the lightning." Ben straightened up in the seat a little and focused on the road ahead. He cast a glance in the rearview mirror to see how Emma was doing after their hasty departure. But she was stretched out longways across the bench seat with her sleeping bag pulled over her. Sam had given up on staking out a spot on the bench seat and climbed up onto her bed atop the gear in the back. Bajer was curled up on the floor as close as she could get to Emma's head.

"Em, you all right, sweetie?" Ben asked.

"I'm fine." Emma's response was muffled and short. Ben decided not to press her further, even though he knew she wasn't fine. But until they got back out on the highway or farther down the road, she was in the safest possible position. Ben had meant to work out different arrangements for travel with Brad, but those plans had fallen by the wayside in this morning's chaos and he had forgotten all about it.

He thought about how fast the morning had gone downhill after his second cup of coffee. Maybe sleeping in the rain last night wouldn't have been so bad if the alternative to what happened this morning had been waking up at a peaceful campsite in the woods somewhere. Of course, it was easy to think like that after enjoying the comfort of a mattress for the night. If dealing with meth head looters was the price to pay for not waking up in the middle of the night because there was a rock poking him in the back, it wasn't worth it.

The exit ramp leading back out onto the highway wasn't far ahead now, and Martin had already started to steer the Scout into the far-right lane. In single file, the other vehicles veered to the right and followed the Scout's lead through the exit ramp. Ben checked the rearview mirror one more time before his view behind them was blocked. What he saw sent cold chills down his spine.

There were at least two vehicles on the road behind them. They hadn't been there a few seconds ago, like they had appeared out of thin air. Ben stepped on the gas and the big Chevy lurched forward.

"What is it?" Sandy could tell something was wrong.

"We've got company." Ben was sure the cars following them had something to do with the two looters who ran away. He stuck his arm out the window and signaled for Joel to pick up his radio.

"Come in, Joel. Over." Ben waited impatiently for Joel to answer, while Sandy repositioned herself in the seat to get a better view of the cars pursuing them.

"Do you think they're after us? They're still way back there," Sandy asked.

"Go ahead. Over," Joel finally answered before Ben had a chance to respond to Sandy.

"We've got a couple vehicles after us. Over." Ben looked at Sandy and then back at Emma before casting a quick glance out the rear window. They were too far around the exit to see the other vehicles now. Ben answered Sandy's question. "Yeah, they're definitely after us, and I'm pretty sure it's got something to do with the two that ran away."

"What do we do? Can we outrun them? Over." Joel's voice crackled over the radio. Ben wasn't sure how best to handle this, but the more he thought about it, the more he realized trying to outrun them wasn't the answer.

"I don't think outrunning them is the answer. Over." They would only be able to go as fast as Rita could drive, and Ben knew her limits. A high-speed chase was more than the old couple could handle. Best-case scenario, they'd end up with a broken-down vehicle, but a bad accident would be a more likely outcome of trying to outrun the looters.

"When you get to the top of the ramp, try to signal the others and get them to stop on the overpass. Grab your weapons and plenty of ammo and be ready. Over."

"Copy that. Over." Ben could hear the worry in Joel's voice, and it was justified. They had no choice but to stand their ground and fight once again.

· 14 ·

Ben was at least grateful for the advantage afforded by the higher position of the overpass. They would have a commanding view of the highway below, and their pursuers would have to drive right underneath them to give chase. The downside was the looters would be on top of them in seconds if they managed to make it to the exit ramp and up to the overpass. Ben didn't particularly care for any of their options, but taking a position and holding their ground was the lesser of two evils.

Ben heard Joel's horn and saw the lights on the Jeep flicker as he tried to get the others' attention. By the time Ben came off the exit ramp, the Scout, Toyota, and Jeep were all stopped in a row along the concrete divider separating the two lanes of the overpass. He pulled in behind them and stopped abruptly, throwing the Blazer into park but leaving it running. He hoped it was a safety measure that wouldn't be needed.

"Grab your rifle and follow me." Ben looked at Sandy before turning toward the back of the truck. "Em, I need you to stay here with the dogs, and no matter what happens, stay down." Emma had come out from under the sleeping bag when Ben first realized they were being chased, but now she was back underneath, with only her head sticking out.

"You hear me? Stay down. There's going to be a lot of shooting, but it's going to be okay. I promise." Ben rubbed the top of her head briefly, but there was no time for further assurances. He grabbed his rifle and slid out of the truck, only reaching back in to grab the three extra box-style magazines for his M24. Joel and the others were outside their vehicles with weapons in hand. Ben yanked a full ammunition can from the bed of the Toyota on his way by the truck.

"You can sit this one out if you want," Ben said as he passed by Rita's open window. The couple hadn't made it out of their vehicle yet, and he didn't see any real advantage to them joining the fight. Besides, he'd rather have them ready to move out if things went south.

Ben was glad to see Martin carrying several extra magazines. So were the kids, including Brad, who was now carrying an AR-15 as well.

"I figured we should all be shooting the same thing, for the ammo." Joel must have seen him eyeing the gun Brad was holding.

Ben nodded. "Good, I want you guys to spread out along the concrete rail and get ready, but don't shoot until I say." Ben pointed to several spots along the edge of the overpass that looked down on the road below. "Brad, can you do me a favor and go keep your sister company?"

"Aw, Dad. Do I have to?" Brad whined.

"Yes, no time to argue. Do it now, please." Ben was stern but did his best to speak calmly even though he knew time was precious right now.

"Fine." Brad turned and stomped toward the Blazer. Ben hated seeing him behave that way, but there was no time to worry about it now. He joined the others along the concrete barricade, finding a spot near the middle between Joel and Sandy. He felt like he could see the whole town from up here. The gas station they'd stopped at yesterday was on the left, and farther down on the right was the motel, still on fire and putting a respectable plume of gray smoke into the otherwise clear blue sky. The smoke would be visible for miles around, and that made him uneasy.

"I see them! Three cars!" Martin shouted from the far end of the line as he watched through the binoculars. Ben propped his rifle up on the concrete barrier and found the first car with his scope. It was an older Ford wagon. Not far behind was a Chevy sedan of some kind, followed at a distance by what looked like a '70s-era mustang hotrod with some body armor crudely welded on. Ben immediately thought back to the white truck that had given them a run for their money through Indiana on their way east. The encounter was the likely cause of the Blazer's breakdown and another reason Ben wanted to avoid a high-speed chase.

The cars were still a good half mile or more from the exit as he watched them weave a path along the wreck-littered road. He had definitely been spotted by the looters, and based on the way they were driving, there was no question now in his mind that they were being pursued.

"When do we shoot?" Martin anxiously worked the charging handle on his AR-15.

"Not yet." Ben tried to anticipate the erratic movements of the approaching cars but found it hard to put his crosshairs on target. Not only were the cars being driven poorly because the occupants were tweaked out on God knew what kind of drugs, but they were also trying to navigate through the maze of obstacles on the road. Ben was hoping to eliminate at least one of the cars, if not two, before they reached the exit, but he wondered if that was going to be possible.

He would have to wait until they came a little closer. Suddenly, the pale blue Chevy, second in line, cut it too close to one of the wrecks and smashed through it with the front corner. To Ben's disappointment, it only slowed the car temporarily, and with one of its headlights now dangling by a wire, it gradually picked up speed again.

Ben focused on the lead car in line. Finding the hood first, he worked his way back to the driver, who was wearing a white T-shirt like one of the three assailants who visited the motel this morning. Ben exhaled slowly. There would be no more warning shots today.

Boom!

He worked the custom bolt on his rifle without a second thought while remaining zeroed in on the car as best as he could. The Ford swerved almost simultaneously, and he wasn't sure if it was due to the shot or something in the road. He had his answer soon, though, and the rough hole in the glass to the left of the driver told him all he needed to know. He prepared to fire again.

Crack...crack...crack! Ben turned to his left to see Joel squeeze off the last of three rounds. Then Martin followed. As did both Allie and Sandy. The others had taken his shot as an indicator to open fire; he should have been more specific with them. Joel was the only one with an optic, and at this distance, he was probably the only one with a decent chance of hitting his intended target. Ben thought about trying to get them to stop, but he wasn't sure he could. Instead, he decided to join them in sending a barrage of lead toward their pursuers. *Let them fight. This is their battle, too.*

Ben heard the first magazine hit the blacktop after only a short while of shooting; it was Martin. No surprise, really. But then Sandy dropped a magazine, a thirty-round one at that.

"Pace yourselves," Ben shouted above the gunfire. They had a lot of ammunition thanks to the weapons cache they discovered at the moonshiners' compound, but being flush with ammunition didn't mean they should burn through more than necessary on this bridge. Ben took a few more shots and emptied his second five-round magazine before pausing to assess the situation. He let the others continue shooting for a few seconds longer before calling out a ceasefire.

The first car had long ago come to a complete stop. Resting sideways across the road and riddled with bullet holes, it almost blocked the entire lane. The driver was slumped over the wheel and without question dead. Ben dropped his empty magazine and slammed the third into place as he watched the Chevy continue the pursuit. One of the vehicle's tires had been shot out and shredded itself off the rim, causing a shower of sparks to be thrown off in its wake as it limped along at half its original speed. The car no longer posed an immediate threat, at least not one worth spending ammunition on at the moment. They could afford to watch and let things play out from the safety of the overpass.

As the Chevy passed the lead car and the dead driver, the sparks from the bare rim ignited a pool of gasoline that had leaked out of the bullet-ridden Ford and snaked its way across the road. The flames traveled back to the source and ignited the gas tank, instantly causing an explosion that shattered the remaining glass in both vehicles.

The Chevy kept moving after the explosion, but not for long, rolling toward the median and stopping several feet into the overgrown weeds.

As soon as the shooting started, the modified Mustang bringing up the rear had slowed down and held back from the others and the overpass by a few hundred yards. The car was out of range for the .223-chambered ARs, or at least far enough away not to take any real damage unless someone got a lucky shot off. After the explosion, the driver brought the vehicle broadside to the road, indicating he had changed his mind about pursuing them, but that wasn't good enough for Ben.

Why did the bad people outnumber the good by so many? Was it because the moral minority were scared to show their faces, or were the delinquents better survivors because they were readily willing to do the bad things to endure these times? One thing was clear. For Ben, there was no more internal turmoil. Gone was the doubt about deserved or not deserved. There were wicked people everywhere, and Ben no longer cared to try and make a distinction between the just and unjust.

This world was what they made of it for themselves, and one less bad guy was always a good thing.

Boom! Ben took the shot, but the bullet missed the thin slot in the metal panel, hitting just above the opening and disappearing in a cloud of rust vibrated loose by the impact. The Mustang spun its tires and launched into a couple of 360-degree burnouts in the middle of the road while Ben chambered another round. The car came to a stop with the passenger side facing the overpass, and the door popped open for a split second while the passenger flashed a rude gesture in their direction before quickly closing the door.

Ben made a slight adjustment to the scope and exhaled slowly.

Boom! The shot was on the money this time and sailed through the narrow opening in the steel plating that covered the window. Through the crudely cut slot, Ben saw the passenger drop from sight as the Mustang spun its tires once again, only this time it was to turn around and speed off in the opposite direction. The only remorse Ben felt was for not hitting the driver with his first attempt.

· 15 ·

Ben stood up from his crouched position behind the concrete barrier as the Mustang hightailed it out of range.

"Is everyone all right?" Ben glanced to his left and right as the others stood up from their positions. The looters hadn't fired a single shot at them. Not that he'd noticed, anyway.

"We're fine." Joel spoke for himself and Allie.

"Do you think they'll come back with more cars?" Martin asked.

"I don't think so." But Ben wasn't sure. After that display of firepower, the remaining looters might think twice about pursuing them any farther. Sandy silently leaned against the concrete guardrail while staring out toward Falls Creek.

Ben approached her quietly while the kids and Martin slowly returned to the vehicles, making small talk about what had just happened.

"Hey, you okay?" Ben placed his hand on Sandy's shoulder and startled her. "Sorry."

"Oh, it's fine." She resumed surveying the scene left behind by the recent battle. The blue Chevy sedan was no longer recognizable, completely engulfed in flames. Black smoke poured from the windows and rose into the now not-so-clear morning sky.

"Do you ever get the feeling none of this is real, like we're living in some kind of dream, a bad dream?" she added.

"I know what you mean." Ben stood next to her, watching the car burn. The gasoline had set some of the tall grass ablaze, and Ben imagined the whole median strip would be on fire soon. The ground was still damp from last night's rain, but the dry brown weeds made good tinder.

He wanted to give Sandy the time she needed to process this in her own way, and as badly as he wanted to move away from this area, he decided to give her a few minutes. He squeezed her shoulder before heading for the truck.

"We're ready when you are. Take your time," he said.

Crouching down on the hard blacktop hadn't done his knee any favors, and he tried to put as much weight on his good knee as he could without drawing attention to himself. Thankfully, the others were gathered around the Toyota, filling Rita and Carlos in on what happened.

Ben was surprised when Sandy came over and insisted on helping him. "You're still in bad shape, huh? Here, lean on me. That's what we're here for, right? To lean on each other?" She flashed the hint of a smile.

"That's right." Ben was glad to see Sandy had moved on, at least enough to set her emotions aside for now. They needed to get moving before the smoke and gunfire attracted anyone else, although after the amount of destruction they had unleashed on the looters, he was thinking it might be a deterrent to some degree. And for the first time, Ben realized that when they stood together, armed, they were a force to be reckoned with. He was proud of their toughness, and although what they were having to go through wasn't something he would have ever wished for, it seemed to be bringing out the best in all of them.

"All right, guys, let's get this show on the road. Don't want to hang around here any longer than we need to. Same vehicle order as yesterday." Just because they were well armed and successful at holding off the looters didn't mean he wanted to test their abilities again anytime soon. He was sure trouble would find them easily enough without invitation.

"What's the goal for today? How far do you think we'll make it?" Allie asked.

"Depending on the road conditions and how

thirsty the Scout proves to be, we should be able to cross over into Ohio in about four hours or so." Ben had scaled the distance on the atlas last night before bed, and he figured the actual distance to the state line was around 115 miles. That would have normally taken about two hours, but the word "normal" had lost all meaning long ago.

"Yeah, you probably want to go a little easier on the Scout. Every time you get on it, we have a hard time breathing in the Jeep." Joel glanced at Martin and laughed, but there was a lot of truth to what he was saying, and it brought up something Ben had been meaning to talk to the man about.

"Not only that, but we need to conserve gas. Every time we stop for fuel, it puts us at risk for stuff like that." Ben glanced over at the plume of black smoke just beyond the overpass, then back at Martin.

Martin held both hands up in the air. "Point taken. Say no more. It does sound good, though, doesn't it?"

"Yes, but every time it *sounds good*, you're probably using half a gallon of gas. We need to see what type of range the Scout has today under *normal* driving conditions. That way, we can plan our stops better if possible." Ben exaggerated a little on the gas usage, but he was trying to scare Martin, and it needed to be said. They had already wasted enough time talking; there was no need to mince words.

Ben turned to walk away but stopped. There was one more thing he wanted to say. "If you're not driving, let's work on getting the magazines reloaded." The others nodded in agreement as they all separated for their vehicles.

Joel stopped. "What about Brad? Is he riding with you now?" Before Ben had a chance to respond, Brad appeared from around the far side of the Blazer.

Ben thought about it for a minute as the three of them looked at each other. Brad was already disappointed he'd been assigned to stay with his sister during the skirmish.

Ben shrugged. "It's your choice."

Joel hesitated for a second. "Well, come on then."

"Thanks, Dad." Brad smiled and shouldered his AR while running to catch up to his brother.

"Joel, you take the lead today. We'll bring up the rear." It was the least he could do, and as confidently as he'd told Martin the looters wouldn't continue chasing them, he couldn't help but wonder if they would see that Mustang again. If it showed up in anyone's rearview mirror, he'd rather it be his. Ben shook his head as he approached the Blazer and met Sandy's gaze.

"What?" she asked.

"I don't want to hear about it. I lost my shot at the father-of-the-year award a while ago. Don't you think?" Ben joked.

"Oh, I think the exact opposite, actually. By the way, have fun loading magazines." Sandy cut him off on his way to the driver's side of the truck. He couldn't argue, not with the way he was carrying himself.

Sam and Bajer were all noses as he climbed into the truck. Both dogs had pushed their way over the center console to greet them upon their return.

"All right, all right." Ben acknowledged each of them with a quick rub on the head. "Back up now. Go on, back up." He noticed Emma was out from under the sleeping bag, but probably because of the temperature more than anything.

"Come on, here." Emma slapped her hand on the bench seat, and the dogs tried to outmaneuver one another to get next to her. "You know I can take care of myself, Dad. I don't need Brad to watch over me."

"I know, but it makes me feel better knowing where you both are and that you're together. I'm your dad. I'm allowed to worry." Ben hoped that was a good enough reason for right now. It was the truth. He found one of his water bottles and washed down a couple more pills for his knee. "I really appreciate you driving, Sandy."

"No problem. I'm glad to help take some of the load off of you." She began to ease the Blazer out onto the road as she followed Martin in the Scout.

Ben looked back at Emma and smiled as he arranged his M24 in the space between the console and his seat. She seemed content with his earlier answer, at least enough not to pursue it any further, and had buried her face in a book. He was sure she had read it a few times over by now.

"Maybe we could keep our eyes out for a library or a bookstore that's still standing and find you some new books to read." Ben glanced back at Emma once more.

"Oh yeah, that's a good idea. I wouldn't mind finding something myself. Reading is such a great escape," Sandy added.

In spite of their enthusiasm, a simple "yeah" was the only response they got from Emma, but Ben would take it over her complaining any day. Considering what they had just been through and witnessed, he was impressed overall that the conversation after the firefight hadn't been full of questions and uncertainty.

Gone were the days of thinking that maybe they'd endured their last encounter with trouble before they reached home. That had always been something he'd clung to, no matter how unlikely, but that hope had vanished, along with their chances of avoiding future conflicts. As those who survived began to emerge from hiding, their number of encounters would increase. And while they wouldn't all be bad people, there would be no shortage of those who sought to do them harm and take what they had.

Ben adjusted himself in the seat and watched the Scout for a minute or two before dumping a few boxes of .223 onto the open road atlas in his lap. He began loading the empty magazines as he thought about what the day might hold for them. In some ways, not knowing what would try to do them in today, recent troubles excluded, was the hardest part. They'd seen more action in the last few days than they had all trip.

He wanted nothing more than to chisel away at the mileage standing between them and home, but reaching Colorado was starting to feel more like their secondary objective. Their first had become staying alive.

· 16 ·

It wasn't even eight o'clock in the morning yet and Ben could already feel the intensity of the sun's rays on his arm resting out the window. It was going to be another scorcher, maybe the hottest day yet. With clear skies as far as they could see in every direction, there would be no relief from the sun today while they traveled.

They'd have to pace themselves and keep an eye on the vehicles so they didn't overheat. Ben wished he'd mentioned the possibility of overheating to Martin; hopefully the guy knew enough to watch his gauges. The Scout worried Ben the most, but that had as much to do with the driver as it did with the vehicle. Ideally, Martin would take their little talk to heart and amend his bad habits behind the wheel. But there was no guarantee against mechanical failure, a constant anxiety Ben had learned to live with.

He watched the convoy of trucks snake around

the hollowed-out and blackened frame of a delivery truck blocking half of the road, the Jeep leading the way. Rita and Carlos were next in line, and as Ben expected, Rita slowed the Toyota down more than necessary in order to navigate around the wreck, which took up the better part of the right-hand lane.

He'd noticed Rita's lack of confidence yesterday with some of the driving, but what choice did they have? Her husband was still too weak to take the wheel, and if Allie took over driving the Toyota again, Joel would be alone with his little brother and Carlos. Ben liked the idea of Allie riding in the Jeep with the boys. She was a competent shot and a level head when the chips were down. Additionally, the two of them made a good team, and it did Ben good to see them together. They had both lost so much, and with so many things beyond their control these days, Ben felt like the least he could do was give them time together. They were clearly in love, and it was a bright spot in an otherwise bleak world that for the most part lacked civility.

Besides, the older couple would have to go it alone eventually when it came time to part ways, which Ben thought might be as soon as sometime tomorrow. But then again, at this rate of speed, it might take longer. The only thing he'd wanted to do this morning was get back on the road as quickly as possible, and now that they were, he wished they could somehow fast-forward and skip the monotony included with a day's worth of slow traveling.

Ben was grateful that Sandy was driving and letting him rest his knee. He made sure to move it around once in a while, at least as much as he could in the confines of the passenger seat. He finished loading the empty magazines and stacked them neatly in the center console, along with the road atlas. He'd studied the map so much lately he felt that he could finish the trip without it, including the detours he planned around the larger cities.

Youngstown, Ohio, was the next major city they would have to deal with. Ben was hoping to skirt by to the north. According to the map, the interstate appeared to run far enough outside the city limits to satisfy him. He had begun to reconsider, however, and based on this morning's events, he thought a more northerly route would be wiser. If there was a growing number of survivors out and about, it would be in their best interest to avoid the more populated areas, even if it meant going a little farther out of their way.

Avoiding people had been their plan from the start, but he felt it was more important now than ever to make sure they did their best to abide by that rule. They'd gotten complacent on the trip east, passing through many towns along the way without seeing a soul. Ben feared those days were over, and even worse, the people they encountered from here on out were going to be desperate, and desperation could drive a person to do anything in the name of survival. As much as he liked to think they'd seen the worst of their trip so far, something told him they hadn't.

Ben leaned to the left and then rocked back the other way with the Blazer as Sandy steered around a small accident. A newer-model Jeep, like his back in Durango, had been rear-ended by a small sedan of some sort. The car was wedged halfway under the Jeep, the result of a high-speed impact. Ben imagined the Jeep dying when the EMPs hit and then sitting dead on the road in the foggy early-morning hours. The sedan's engine held out a little longer for whatever reason and came up on the Jeep out of nowhere. Judging by the lack of tire marks on the road, Ben thought the sedan never even hit the brakes.

The driver and passenger of the car must have died instantly, and from the looks of things, they were the lucky ones. The sedan had forced the front end of the small SUV off the road and into the median, causing a piece of guardrail to peel up and skewer the Jeep's windshield. Remarkably, neither car had burned, like so many others, and the lack of a fire was what had initially drawn Ben's attention.

But as they passed, something else caused him to stare. Two cracked and bloody spots on the punctured windshield indicated the driver and passenger of the Jeep hadn't fared too well. The swarm of flies hovering near the busted-out windows confirmed it.

Sandy gave the blazer a little gas as she straightened out the wheel. Ben turned a little in the seat. For some reason, he couldn't bring himself to look away. Eventually, the wreck became obscured from view by overgrown vegetation. With some of the weeds reaching as high as the windows on the Jeep, it looked like it had been sitting there for years rather than weeks.

Ben wondered if there had been any passengers in the back of either vehicle or if anyone survived. It was possible, since the cars hadn't caught on fire. It was a testament to the times they were living in, though, that his initial instinct was to feel worse for the people who had possibly made it out alive than for those who perished immediately upon impact. He couldn't imagine the survivors making it far on foot in this heat, especially if they were wounded. With no help for miles around, it wouldn't end well for anyone who managed to walk away.

"You never really get used to it, do you?" Sandy noticed him watching the wreck as they passed.

"No, not really. Strange that the cars weren't burned, though."

"Yeah, I noticed that, too."

"I guess it's a good thing, right? Not getting used to seeing things like that." Sandy glanced at the rearview mirror.

"Yeah, some days I notice it more than others." Ben checked on Emma, who was still reading. She'd mastered the art of ignoring the outside world, and Ben was a little jealous at times. Sam had resigned herself to the makeshift bed among the gear in the back, and Bajer was stretched out across the seat with her head resting on Emma's leg. The poor dog was so thankful to have been rescued from the moonshiners' compound she might never let Emma out of her sight again.

When he turned around, Ben was glad to see the silhouette of a large highway sign up ahead. Sandy repositioned her hands on the wheel and sat up a little. She seemed just as happy to see the sign. It was the first one they'd seen since leaving Falls Creek, and Ben was anxious to see actual mileage for some of the places they had to pass through. He'd given up on the mile markers some time ago. They'd slowed down too many times, and he couldn't read the numbers off the ones he'd been able to pick out among the weeds.

He knew approximately where they should be, but it would be nice to know how many miles they had to go until they could leave this state behind. They'd been here far too long and were worse off for it. Ben was almost afraid to read the sign out of fear he would be disappointed with how little progress they had made so far today. He knew they'd been averaging between forty-five and fifty-five miles per hour on the open sections of highway, but there were also plenty of times when he glanced over at the speedometer and saw it hovering below twenty while they navigated through some of the more congested sections.

What concerned him the most, though, was the fact that they hadn't passed by Brookeville yet. It was the next closest town on the map, and according to his measurements, it shouldn't have been too much farther.

"Brookville exit, two miles. Ninety-five miles to Youngstown, Ohio." Ben read the sign out loud. It was worse than he thought. He looked at his watch and re-ran the numbers in his head.

"What's wrong?" Sandy asked.

"That can't be right." Ben ran his hand through his hair and sighed. "We've gone less than thirty miles in the last hour."

"Is that all? I thought we'd been driving for a lot longer." Sandy sounded as disappointed about the time as he was about the mileage, and rightfully so. Ben heard Emma sigh loudly from the back seat. Unless something changed, this was going to be a much longer day than he anticipated. They were still deep in the foothills of the Appalachians.

Maybe the road would open up a bit more. As it was, with the other side of the highway being unreachable due to the heavily forested and over-grown median, they were limited to the westbound lanes of travel.

Of course, when the landscape did open up more and start to flatten out, they would lose what little shade they had been enjoying through some of the denser sections of trees. There weren't many leaves on the trees, but the dead foliage still clinging to the branches, along with the thinner but more resilient pines, provided sporadic relief from the direct sunlight. However, the constant flashes of light caused by the sun passing behind the trees created a hypnotic effect, and Ben felt himself getting drowsy on a few occasions already this morning. But he refused to leave Sandy alone and fought the urge to nap.

Ben went over the math in his head a few times and guessed they were likely to end up somewhere between Youngstown and Akron. And he could live with that, mostly because it would put them at the separation point from Rita and Carlos in the middle of the day tomorrow. The reasoning was selfish, but he'd feel less guilty sending the older couple off on their own in broad daylight than close to dark. And it would alleviate him and the others from feeling obligated to stop and spend another night before parting ways, if it was early enough in the day.

It wasn't that he meant Rita or her husband any ill-will. Quite the opposite, in fact. In some ways, they even reminded Ben of his own parents. They were very friendly and got along well with the group, but every time he saw the Toyota's brake lights and felt their convoy slow, his desire to prolong their involvement with the couple any longer than necessary began to wane.

Ben tried to stop thinking about schedules and wasted time. Stressing over their speed, or lack thereof, wouldn't change anything. He tried to tell himself, like he had in the past, that it was better to be cautious and safe than fast. But repeating that mantra didn't seem to quell the anxiety he felt about their traveling arrangements. The only thing he didn't need convincing of was that it was going to be a rough day if he kept beating himself up over their current situation.

Ben tried to focus on the forest that surrounded them. It wouldn't be long before they'd be back out on the flatlands of the Midwest. And although it seemed like they would never get there at their current rate of travel, he knew what lay ahead, and that worried him to some degree as well.

Their current location was the farthest north they would be on this trip, and if it were this hot and dry at this latitude, what was the climate like farther south? It was already the end of June, and the temperatures weren't getting any cooler.

This was the first time Ben had given serious consideration to the possibility of taking a different way home.

After Cloverdale, they could stay on I-70 until just before St. Louis, then turn north and follow the upper Mississippi River until they hit I-80 again. That would mean driving through Iowa and Nebraska, but the higher elevations meant cooler weather, and the desolate areas they would be traveling through were a bonus. A northern route would certainly add a few days to their trip, but it might make for a better experience. Their chances of finding fresh water and food were more likely, as they would intersect with some major rivers along the way.

The new plan would take them through uncharted territory as well. But based on the trouble they ran into along I-70, that wasn't a big concern. Ben could certainly do without being reminded of some of the challenges they faced traveling east. And he was sure the kids would agree. He'd have to give it some more thought and then maybe talk it over with the others when they stopped for lunch.

"Why don't you try to get some rest?" Sandy adjusted her sitting position.

"I'm okay."

"Well, I'm going to need a break driving at some point later today, so you might as well—"

"Wait. Sorry, but do you hear that?" Ben held up his finger. The truck's exhaust sounded different, and he couldn't tell if they were having mechanical problems or if Martin was back to his old tricks. But the Scout remained at a steady pace and the noise wasn't coming from in front of them.

Sandy checked the instrument panel. "Everything looks fine."

Ben turned in his seat to see if the Blazer was putting off any smoke. He wasn't sure what he expected to see, but it certainly wasn't the armor-clad Mustang pulling out from behind the last wreck they'd passed. He recognized the sound now, and as the Mustang started to speed up, Ben's heart sank. He knew in his gut they hadn't seen the last of that car, but he was really hoping to be wrong for once.

· 17 ·

Ben really regretted missing the shot he had at the driver, especially now that the Mustang was back on their tails. But this was no time to think about what he should have done. They needed to come up with a plan to deal with this guy before he caused a serious accident. It was a good thing there was a lot of distance between them still; it gave Ben a little time to think.

He put his hand on Sandy's arm. "Don't panic, but the Mustang is back."

Sandy gasped and started to turn to look behind them, but Ben stopped her. "Just focus on driving. He's a little ways back yet."

Sandy swallowed hard and repositioned her hands on the steering wheel, wrapping her fingers around it tightly as the Blazer began to speed up. They couldn't indulge the Mustang in a high-speed chase, not only because they probably couldn't outrun it, but mainly because Ben was sure they'd end up breaking one of the vehicles—or worse. And even if they wanted to run, there was no way Rita and Carlos would be able to keep up. What were they supposed to do? Leave them behind? That wasn't an option, and he knew it.

"What are we going to do?" Sandy bit her lip as she continuously checked the rearview mirror.

"I want you to slow down." Ben spoke as calmly as he could.

"You what?" Sandy glanced at him, then back at the road, a line etched between her brows.

"Slow down. We have to keep him from getting past us and reaching the others. Em, honey, I want you back down on the seat, flat, and call Sam down with you." Ben rattled off instructions without looking up from his M24. He inserted a freshly loaded magazine and tried not to think about how none of this would be happening had they been driving faster.

Emma was already lying down across the bench seat and trying to coax Sam to join her. The big yellow dog resisted leaving her nest but quickly moved out of the way when she realized Ben was moving to the back of the truck.

"Get on the radio to Joel and let him know what's going on. Tell him to pick up the pace a little but not so much he loses Rita. We need them to get ahead of us so we have space to maneuver. So *you* have space." Ben and Sandy locked eyes for a moment in the rearview mirror. "You can do this." Sandy looked away, and Ben crawled the rest of the way over the seat and took a prone position across the gear. He was thankful for the cushy dog bed under his ribs. Using his left foot, he braced himself against the back of the passenger seat and searched for the Mustang in his scope.

In the background, Ben heard Sandy and Joel chatter back and forth over the radio and recognized the tone of Joel's voice immediately.

"Just tell him I said do it. No arguments." Ben needed to concentrate, and he could do that better knowing Joel was doing what he had been asked and leading the others away from the maniac behind them. There was no time for arguments or heroics. This was about eliminating a threat the safest and quickest way possible. And that was just what Ben intended on doing.

"This is gonna get loud. Might want to cover your ears." The warning was more for Emma, who had the ability to block out the sound. Sandy would need to keep her hands on the wheel, but Ben wanted her to be ready as well.

Shooting the .338 Lapua from inside the truck was going to be a little jarring, to say the least. Even with the windows open, they were all destined to go to bed tonight with ringing in their ears. He inched his way toward the back of the truck and pushed the muzzle out beyond the rear window and the cab of the Blazer. It was the best he could do to help mitigate the impending shockwave of kinetic energy he was about to unleash.

He wished there was time to pull over and get set up in a proper shooting position; this would be a hard shot on a good day. Between the necessary maneuvers Sandy was making to avoid abandoned vehicles on the road and the deliberate zigzagging of the Mustang, it was extremely difficult to get a fix on the thin slots cut in the armor. Ben tried to steady himself as the Blazer took a rough bounce.

Boom! Ben took the shot but knew it was off before he saw the sparks fly from the metal plating. The only thing louder than the gun was Emma's scream as the Blazer jerked to the left and then corrected course just as fast.

"Sorry," Sandy apologized.

"Cover your ears," Ben shouted over the wind rushing through the truck. Sandy was inadvertently speeding up again. He didn't blame her. It went against any sane person's instinct to slow down when being chased, but speed wasn't the answer here. Good, smooth driving and solid, deliberate actions behind the wheel would get them through this. And Emma needed to cover her ears if she was going to scream every time he took a shot and cause Sandy's driving to suffer.

"You're doing great, but we need to slow down a little," Ben called out.

"I'm trying," she answered. Ben settled in for another shot at the Mustang and felt the Blazer slow. He tried to focus on the front tires, not because he didn't want to kill the driver, but because he thought he might have a better chance at doing some damage capable of stopping the chase. Ben winced as Sandy hit a rough spot on the road and something sharp poked into his rib through the dog bed. As soon as the road smoothed out, he resumed lining up his shot.

There was no shot, though. And as he zeroed in on the right front tire, he saw that the Mustang had a steel plate welded to the front bumper, leaving only an inch or so between the pavement and the armor. Trying to take out a tire through that small of an opening wouldn't be any easier than getting a shot through the slit in front of the driver. He tried his best to anticipate the bumps in the road, but it was impossible.

Boom! He knew his aim was off but took the shot anyway, if for no other reason than to let the driver of the Mustang know they weren't letting up. Ben expected Emma to scream again and glanced backward while cycling the rifle bolt, but she was quiet this time. He was encouraged to see the back end of the Scout so far ahead of them. With the others a couple hundred yards away, it gave Sandy a little breathing room to maneuver the Blazer. But the feeling didn't last long, disappearing altogether when he met Sandy's gaze in the rearview mirror. He recognized the expression on her face.

"Two more!" He didn't get what she meant at first but understood immediately when he turned his attention back toward the Mustang and saw that two motorcycles had joined the chase. *This just keeps getting better.* The bikes had appeared out of nowhere, and it took his brain a moment to acknowledge that what he was seeing was real.

"Em, I need you to pass me the AR-15 and a couple mags from the console." What Ben needed now was quantity, not quality. He considered using the Kel-Tech, but the motorcycles were too far back for the shotgun to be effective, even with the Dragon's Breath rounds. To the bikers, both of whom were heavily protected with helmets and what he recognized as low-grade body armor, a shot from the 12-gauge would feel no worse than driving through a swarm of flies. Ben wasn't sure if they had steel inserts in place, but he was anxious to find out and would have already if it weren't for the additional protection on the bikes themselves.

The motorcycles fit right in with the Mustang, with steel plates and other sharpened pieces of metal welded to their shrouds and frames wherever possible. Not only were the modifications intimidating to look at, but they also created a cocoon of armor that all but obscured the riders from his perspective. The bikers weren't as well protected as their partner in the car, but landing a decent shot would still be challenging, given the bikes' agility.

"Em—" Ben started to yell but stopped when he felt the butt of the AR-15 poking him in his side.

"Here." Emma passed the rifle over the seat, followed by four thirty-round magazines he had just loaded earlier.

"Thanks," he said, but she was gone, back under the sleeping bag with the dogs on the floor of the truck. Ben pushed the M24 aside and slapped a magazine into the AR-15. He wouldn't have the accuracy of the .338, but that was proving to be a waste in these conditions anyway. Maybe he'd have more luck convincing their pursuers that this was a bad idea with the .223. With the freshly loaded magazines by his side, he had 120 good reasons why they should turn around.

But this wasn't just a random bunch of looters. The Mustang and the bikes were too well set up to terrorize and intimidate unsuspecting travelers. These guys were well-practiced highway bandits, and they weren't going to stop until Ben and the others were dead.

· 18 ·

"It's gonna get loud in here." Ben tried to give the girls a heads-up, but he was afraid no amount of warning could prepare them for the assault he was about to unleash on their hearing. The AR-15 had a much shorter barrel than the M24, preventing him from pushing the muzzle much past the rear window. He was already closer to the edge of the tailgate than he wanted to be. As it was, he felt like he was on the verge of sliding out the back of the truck and onto the blacktop rushing by below him. It didn't help matters any with Sandy picking up speed again.

Pop, pop, pop. The anticipated sharp crack of the AR-15 was absent, replaced by a much louder report that Ben felt in his chest with each pull of the trigger. The empty shell casings rattled off the side window of the Blazer's cab while he did his best to ignore them and focus on the target.

The first three rounds sent sparks off the leading

motorcycle's shroud, causing the bike to swerve sharply and glance off the side of the Mustang as it tried to pass. Ben thought the bike was going down, but he was disappointed to see the rider recover control and steady the machine just in time to avoid colliding with the remains of an abandoned pickup truck along the edge of the road.

Pop, pop, pop...pop, pop, pop. Two more short bursts put the bike into peril once more, only this time, Ben didn't let up. He emptied the rest of the magazine as fast as he could while maintaining control and staying on target. He felt the empty casings bounce off his body and ricochet around the inside of the truck. A few found their way down the collar of his shirt and burned him where they settled, but he was too focused on making his shots count to let it bother him. It was a small price to pay to help even the odds a little.

The rider seemed to have survived the barrage of bullets relatively unscathed, but the same couldn't be said for his bike. Ben could see a trail of fluids behind the bike, and the rider was rapidly losing his ability to control the machine. Ben watched it all unfold in slow motion.

The front wheel of the bike began to wobble uncontrollably until it was sideways enough to bite the blacktop and send the bike diving into the left-hand lane. The rider went down hard and separated from the bike upon impact but followed behind in a short slide that left a trail of parts strewn across the blacktop.

Ben wasn't sure if the accident had killed the man or not, but it didn't matter; if he were still alive, the Mustang barreling toward him at full speed would finish the job. Maybe the driver couldn't see very well through the small slits in the Mustang's windshield, or maybe he intended on hitting the downed rider and bike at full speed, but Ben never saw any indication of the Mustang slowing down.

The lower plate welded onto the Mustang's cowl acted like a plow, smashing through all but the smaller pieces of debris scattered along the road. The unsuspecting driver was next, and Ben looked away for a moment right before the car came into contact with the downed man. When he looked back, the body was wedged under the front of the Mustang and slowly but surely being forced through the one-inch gap at the bottom of the steel plate as the vehicle continued forward. The helmet was the only recognizable thing after several yards of the biker being dragged across the blacktop at speed. Refusing to give way and get sucked under the car, it hung on stubbornly.

To Ben, it looked like the old Ford sped up right before slamming into the bike. Maybe the driver had hoped to hit the motorcycle with enough force to plow right through the wreckage and continue the chase. The Mustang shuddered as the front end grappled with the sudden mass of an armored motorcycle under the front bumper. Unlike the flesh and bone of the rider, the bike refused to pass quietly under the Mustang, throwing sparks in every direction.

Ben was encouraged to see the car slowing down as it struggled to deal with the wreckage, the remaining pieces wedging themselves farther beneath the undercarriage with each passing moment. The remaining rider held back and coasted behind the Mustang, but Ben wasn't taking any chances. He slapped a new magazine into place and charged the weapon as he searched for the other bike in his sights.

Pop, pop, pop...pop, pop, pop. Ben stopped after the second burst and watched the remains of the already downed bike ball up under the Ford and cause the car to launch itself up and over the wreckage. The entire Mustang shook violently, contorting the body of the car in the process, until it landed on the other side of the debris with a crash that shook the front end. The lower piece of armored plating, which had prevented Ben from getting a clean shot at the tires, flew off and skidded ahead of the Mustang.

He was tempted to shoot again but restrained himself. The other bike was stopping to check on the disabled Mustang, and both were fading fast from a decent shooting range.

"It's over," Ben called out. "Will you let Joel know? They can slow down now."

"Got it," Sandy shouted back. Ben was relieved but remained in position. With radio chatter in the background, he watched the smoking Mustang grow smaller on the highway behind them. The driver was out of the car now and walking around with the guy on the bike. Ben was disappointed that neither of them seemed hurt. He felt the Blazer ease into a gentle curve in the highway, and just like that, the Mustang was gone from sight.

"Joel wants to know if they should stop somewhere up ahead and wait." Sandy held the radio in one hand and kept the other on the wheel.

"No, no stopping. We'll catch up to them. The Mustang's down but not out." Ben started to shimmy backward off the pile of gear and stopped when he reached the back seat. Both dogs stared up at him and wagged their tails as he climbed over them to the center console.

"Em… Emma, honey, it's over." Ben pulled the sleeping bag off her head and saw that she still had her ears covered and her eyes squeezed shut. He touched one of her hands and she jumped.

"Are they gone?" She pulled her hands away from her ears.

"Yes, it's over," Ben assured her as he continued

making his way back into the passenger seat. Emma threw the sleeping bag off as best as she could with the dogs lying on top of her and slowly returned to her seat. Ben could breathe better now that he was back in his seat. The bed they'd made for Sam in the back provided a cushion between the gear and his ribs, but it hadn't done anything for the pain he experienced when drawing in a normal breath while lying in the prone position.

He noticed Sandy was still shaken from the experience and had resumed her death grip on the steering wheel now that she wasn't holding the radio.

He reached over and placed his hand on her shoulder. "You did a good job driving. It's okay to relax for now." Ben noticed the Scout not too far up ahead. He had no idea how Rita had managed to keep up with the others, but it was time to slow down before someone made a mistake.

"For now." Sandy forced out a short laugh. "So do you think they'll be back?"

"Maybe." Ben glanced back at Emma, who met his gaze. "If they can even find us. We'll be long gone before they get back on the road. The car took a lot of damage, and one of the bikers is done for." He stopped himself from listing any more reasons why they were probably safe from the bandits. "But yeah, we need to keep an eye out."

And they did, because the truth was, he didn't

know if the Mustang and bike would be back to bother them again. It was what Emma and Sandy both needed to hear from him. Being up front about things was part of the no-sugarcoating-things deal he'd made with himself when it came to the kids. And after the morning they'd had, it was time to try some of that honesty out.

Emma wasn't interested in her book anymore, and Ben noticed her attention was mostly directed out her window and occasionally behind them. Maybe it was a good thing he wasn't the only one keeping an eye out for trouble. Not that the others weren't on the lookout already, but the possibility of danger would keep them on their toes, and right now, he welcomed the help.

His thoughts kept flashing back to the last image he saw as they went around the corner and lost sight of the broken-down Mustang. The steam escaping from the damaged front end, the driver walking around the car with his hands flailing, no doubt yelling about what had happened to his car and them getting away.

He hoped the damage was catastrophic and the car was beyond repair. The bike was still operational, though, and Ben half expected it to appear behind them at any moment, although he thought it more likely the bandits would fix the Mustang and seek revenge together. Maybe there were more of them and they would return in even greater numbers. But now his imagination was getting the better of him.

If Emma weren't here, he would have asked Sandy to stop, maybe even go back, so he could finish the bandits off. That would have guaranteed no future trouble from either of them, and he wondered if not doing just that was a mistake. Unfortunately, there would be plenty of time to think about all of it over the next few hours of driving and looking over his shoulder.

· 19 ·

It was hard to believe that spending the night in the motel had cost them so much. One thing was for sure: they'd be camping somewhere remote tonight, no matter the weather. It would be a long time before Ben agreed to stay someplace like that again or went against his intuition for the sake of comfort.

The only good thing to come out of their pit stop in Falls Creek was the full tanks of gas he was especially grateful for. Considering what had just happened, it was nice to be able to drive for a while without worrying about having to stop for fuel.

Eventually, Emma went back to reading her book, and Bajer found a spot for her head on Emma's lap. Sam had returned to her bed on top of the gear and was snoring loudly. Even the dogs seemed to know it was going to be a while before they stopped again.

The highway began to open up with wider

shoulders and a third lane, allowing them to avoid obstacles with greater ease. Even Rita seemed to be growing more confident with each passing mile and was finding her rhythm behind the Jeep as their four-vehicle convoy wound its way westward along the interstate.

They were finally making decent time now, and Ben started to relax a little. They'd been stuck on the smaller mountain roads for so many days in a row he'd forgotten what it was like to drive at these speeds consistently. If they could maintain this pace, they just might make it to Cloverdale in a couple of days.

Ben checked behind them again. He'd probably continue to do so all the way home. He couldn't shake the image of the Mustang pulling out from behind one of the wrecks.

Emma was sleeping again. He hadn't noticed when she'd stopped reading, but he hardly blamed her. With the windows down in an effort to make the heat more bearable, the wind rushing through the Blazer was too loud for them to hold a conversation or focus on a book.

But the noise was a small price to pay to keep themselves and the vehicles cool. The outside sheet metal of the truck was so hot Ben couldn't rest his arm out the window anymore. He would have been worried about the vehicles overheating if they weren't able to keep the air moving like this.

He still found himself looking over at the temperature gauge from time to time when he thought Sandy wasn't paying attention.

Hopefully she didn't notice and think he didn't trust her. It just made him feel better to see things operating within tolerances for himself. He was already having a hard time believing they hadn't had any mechanical trouble yet, with two unknown vehicles that had been sitting for who knew how long inside the compound.

At least Martin was taking it easy on the Scout so far today, although Ben credited that to the morning they'd had, not to Martin. The guy was a work in progress, far removed from his pencil-pushing life in the city. Ben had to keep that in mind and remember to cut him some slack. That was hard to do at times, especially when he put the others in danger. But it would all be worth it when they reached Cloverdale with a truck full of supplies. At least that was what Ben kept telling himself.

He couldn't blame all their misfortune on the decision to travel with the others they'd met at the compound. They probably would have stayed at the motel last night whether they were with Martin and the older couple or not, given the intensity of the storm. Allie's close call with the lightning strike was proof of that.

He wondered if the type of storm they

experienced last night was what they should expect from now on. All the weather seemed more extreme since the EMPs. It was like they had lost a protective layer of the atmosphere. The sun today felt like it was only a couple of miles away, and the shadow lines it caused were so crisp they looked cartoonish.

Today was the first day they'd seen the sky this blue and bright. It reminded him of Colorado, but as refreshing as it was to see clear sky, he'd rather have the clouds and haze they'd grown accustomed to. At least then they would have a buffer from the direct rays of the sun. Until now, he hadn't realized just how much relief the darkened skies had provided.

"Do we have any more water?" Sandy finished the last drops from her Nalgene bottle. Ben pulled a full bottle, one of three remaining, from beneath a pile of towels; he'd stowed them there in an attempt to shelter them from the heat. He missed the days when they were all in the Blazer together and Allie would keep the water cool by wrapping bottles in towels for insulation. She did a better job than him. And with Emma and two dogs climbing all over the place, he wasn't sure why he even bothered trying.

Ben handed the warm bottle to Sandy. "Sorry, that's the best I can do."

"Hey, at least it's wet, right?" She unscrewed the lid and took a few small sips before setting it down.

She did her best to pretend it was refreshing, but the look on her face told a different story. The water situation was starting to concern him; there was just too much going on to think about it before now. Some of the others had not been as frugal with their water supply as he would have liked them to be. Apparently, everyone had used a fair amount of water to get cleaned up last night and again when they were getting ready this morning. Ben hadn't realized how much they'd used exactly because of how quickly they'd left the motel, but he had come to learn over the course of the morning that they were down to less than a few gallons.

He'd been clear—at least he thought he had been—that they needed to conserve what they had. Ben was hoping the water they left the compound with would last them a couple of days. But now they needed to add water to their list of needs. The fact that their supplies had gone warm many miles ago only added insult to injury. But at least now he had something to help pass the time: studying the atlas for a likely water source.

Their best bet, in his opinion, was about an hour away, where the interstate crossed the Allegheny River. Lake Erie sat at the headwaters for the Allegheny and should provide them with plenty of relatively clean, easy-to-filter water. According to his road atlas, the river looked to be fairly wide where they would cross, and that meant a bridge.

It also meant the bridge might be impassable; based on what they'd seen, he was concerned that they might run into another roadblock.

They had two other options to cross the river if the interstate bridge was blocked, and he wasn't crazy about either of them. They could head south and cross at Foxburg, but it was a twenty-mile trip out of their way and it would take them closer to Pittsburgh—or what was left of it. The other choice was only slightly less appealing, and it meant making their way directly through the center of Emlenton, Pennsylvania.

Ben didn't know the town from any of the others on the map, but it looked like a decent-sized municipality. And it was the next closest river crossing if the interstate bridge was a bust. Not ideal, with people seemingly coming out of the woodwork all of a sudden.

He liked the sense of security of having extra supplies, but it came at a cost. That cost was anxiety; it felt like they had targets on their backs. And with four vehicles, there was no way they could slip through town unnoticed in the middle of the day. Maybe the heat would play to their advantage and keep people indoors.

Ben tried not to think about it, but it was hard not to, and deliberating his route helped take his mind off the Mustang and motorcycle he was sure would reappear at any moment.

· 20 ·

It would have been easy to take a nap while Sandy was driving, but Ben's conscience wouldn't let him. After the morning they'd had, he couldn't allow himself that luxury. Emma was having no problem sleeping, however, and he hadn't heard a peep from her in quite a while.

He turned to check on his daughter. Both dogs had been forced to find another place to lie. Emma was stretched out across the rear seat, and to his surprise, she still had the sub-zero-rated sleeping bag draped over her body and pulled up snugly around her neck. He couldn't believe she was comfortable beneath that in this heat.

"Is Emma all right? She's been awfully quiet," Sandy asked.

"She's still sleeping. I can't believe she's under the bag, though. She's going to melt." Ben continued to watch her sleep.

"Maybe you should wake her up and get her to

drink some water." Sandy glanced back at her. "She looks hot."

"I know. I hate to disturb her, but maybe you're right." Ben pulled the sleeping bag away from Emma's face and tried to gently wake her up. "Em... Em, honey, are you okay?" He noticed that her clothes were wet under the sleeping bag, and he pulled the rest of it off right away. "Emma, are you okay?"

He was relieved to see her eyes open as she slowly came to life.

"I'm fine. I was just a little cold." She picked at her T-shirt while struggling to get upright in the seat. As soon as there was room on the bench seat, Bajer jumped up and sat next to Emma, wagging her tail and begging for attention. Sam was more reserved and stayed put on the bed of blankets.

"Might do you some good to get some fresh air. Do you want to sit up here for a while by the window?" Ben offered.

"No, I'm fine."

"Here." Ben handed her a bottle of water.

Emma took a drink but pulled back immediately. "Yuck."

"I know. It's all we have, though. You need to try and drink as much as you can. You lost a lot of water sweating under there." Ben glanced at the sleeping bag, which was now occupied by Bajer, who had made a nest in it after failing to get any attention from Emma. When he looked back at his daughter, he noticed the goosebumps covering her legs and arms.

"I've got a chill." She pulled some of the sleeping bag out from under Bajer and used it to cover her legs before resuming her attempt at downing the warm water. Bajer stood up and made a few circles before sitting back down. Ben put the back of his hand against her forehead. She was hot, no doubt about it, but they all were. He couldn't tell if she had a fever or not. His first thought was of the water they had taken from the compound. Maybe it wasn't as clean as they'd thought. But if that were the case, wouldn't they all be sick?

"What do you think? I can't tell." Ben looked at Sandy, who turned and felt Emma's forehead for a few seconds while keeping one eye on the road.

"Yeah, she's a little warm, but in this heat, it's hard to tell." Sandy returned her attention to driving.

Ben could tell the extra attention was making Emma uncomfortable, so he turned around in his seat. "There's a place coming up we can stop and refill the bottles with fresh, cool water." He glanced back at Emma again. She was looking a little better now that she was sitting up.

"Dad, I'm fine. I'm okay." She made a face and turned her attention to Bajer. He hoped she okay, but his gut told him otherwise. There was no telling what was making her feel bad; it could have been anything. They had all been through the wringer over the past few days, and this morning was no exception.

Sandy shot him a quick smile. "She'll be okay. Might just be a touch of motion sickness. All this swerving back and forth can get to you." But Emma wasn't paying attention to their conversation anymore. Bajer was stretched out, allowing Emma to use her as a table for her drawing notebook. He was glad to see her occupied with something other than staring out the windows at the brown and dying landscape. He was tired of looking at it himself.

"There it is." Sandy nodded at the sign up ahead.

EXIT 45, 1 MILE.

"Isn't that the exit you said we might need to come back to if we couldn't get across the bridge?" Sandy asked.

"Yeah, let's hope we don't have to do that and go through town. I guess we'll find out soon enough. The bridge should only be another mile or two ahead." Ben turned the radio on and set it in one of the cupholders in case Joel needed to get in touch with them. If there was a problem crossing the bridge, he wanted to know right away. There was no need to waste any time trying to figure out what to do. Going back to the exit and taking the route through town wasn't something he wanted to do, but putting it off wouldn't help their situation.

Their priority was quickly becoming water, but his plan was to wait and get it on the western side of the river. It looked less populated and would be a better place to take a short break from driving. His map showed some secondary roads probably used for bridge maintenance or highway crews. They could use them to access the water's edge. From the looks of things, he was guessing they were going to cross over the Allegheny at a pretty high elevation.

As they neared the bridge, the surrounding landscape began to fall away steeply from the highway. Sandy merged into the left lane to avoid a row of orange construction barrels. The two sides of the interstate came together just before the bridge, and the grassy median separating the east- and westbound lanes eventually turned into a thin concrete barrier.

Ben wasn't happy to see one of their lanes closed due to road construction. The construction barriers cut their odds of finding an open lane across the river in half. There was no way around it, though; the lanes under construction were impassable, with bare rebar protruding from the surface.

With the road reduced to two narrow lanes bordered by concrete dividers on both sides, the space already felt tight, but Ben's hopes for crossing sank further when they were funneled into a single lane. The entire bridge was under construction, and both directions of traffic had been joined into one lane meant to be operated by a flagman. He wasn't surprised when the Scout's brake lights lit up and the vehicle came to a stop.

"Come in, Dad. Over."

"Go ahead. Over." Ben shook his head at Sandy. "This can't be good."

"We're gonna have to find another way. Over."

"I'll be right there. Over." Ben opened his door, but there was only enough room between the truck and the concrete divider to open it partway.

"Do you want me to go?" Sandy offered.

"No, I won't be long." Ben slid out through the opening and closed the door so he could make his way to the Jeep. There was less than a couple of feet on either side of the row of vehicles; it was easy to see why the road was blocked ahead. He crossed over to the left side of the lane and prepared to pass the driver's side of the Scout on his way by.

Martin's door opened and he jumped out before Ben could pass. "Looks pretty bad."

"Come on, let's take a look." Martin was already out of the truck, and Ben figured he might as well come along and help out if there was anything they could do to keep moving forward.

"You guys doing all right?" Ben didn't stop as

he walked past the Toyota, but he saw Rita nod through the windshield as he glanced back at the couple.

"Looks like we're going back. There's no way we're getting through here." Joel was standing up high on the doorsill of the Jeep and looking out over the line of burnt-out cars in front of him.

He was right. With the entire bridge reduced to one lane and the rest of it unusable due to construction, they had no options this time.

More than a dozen scorched and blackened cars were lined up bumper to bumper in front of the Jeep. They must have been waiting for their turn to proceed across the bridge when the EMPs hit. The first and last cars in the traffic jam were empty, but that wasn't the case for the vehicles trapped in the middle. The skeletal remains of the victims were still visible through the busted-out windows. Some of the car doors were open; their occupants had attempted to escape a fiery death. The badly charred and decayed bodies a few feet from the open doors proved their struggles were futile.

They couldn't move the cars out of the way—none of them even had tires anymore—and it would take way too much time and effort. But even more than that, Ben didn't want to disturb the bodies. They stood there for a minute, taking it in. It was a grim reminder of how lucky they all were.

Standing here in the blazing-hot sun wasn't

getting them any closer to Colorado, and Ben felt more energy being sucked out of him with every second. There was nothing more to think about.

"All right, let's head back to the last exit. Exit 45. It's only a couple miles back." Ben turned to leave.

"Then what?" Allie called out from inside the Jeep.

Ben pointed upriver. "There, but we'll have to go through a small town to get to it." From where they were, Ben could see the Emlenton bridge and a little of the town. It was just a couple of miles away, as the crow flew.

"That's not too far." Martin held his hand over his eyes to block the sun.

"It's not the distance that worries me. We should stick close together through town, weapons ready. I'll lead the way this time, okay?" The others nodded and Ben turned toward the Blazer.

"Dad...what happened with the guy in the Mustang? Sandy said there were a couple bikers, too," Joel asked.

"I don't think we'll be seeing any more of them. I can tell you about it later if you want. Right now, I just want to get off this bridge." He did his best not to sound rude or dismissive, but this wasn't the place or time to have a conversation. Ben turned and headed for the Blazer before Joel had a chance to respond. They'd been here too long already.

· 21 ·

It took more than a few minutes to back their way out to a point where they could execute a very tight three-point turn and head east toward the exit. The single lane and concrete barricades lining the road on both sides made for a slow extraction from the bridge, and the fact that they were extremely vulnerable while getting turned around wasn't lost on Ben.

The disappointment of not being able to cross the river here was a hard pill to swallow, albeit not an unexpected one, but Ben was happy to be off the bridge and moving at a decent speed again. It felt strange to be heading east and driving down the wrong side of the highway. It made more sense than trying to cross over the median through waist-high or taller vegetation, though. When they'd done it before, it was a calculated risk and the grass was shorter. They could see the larger pieces of debris or wreckage and avoid them, but now there was no telling what was hidden from sight among the overgrowth. It wouldn't take much to puncture a tire or tear something loose from the under-carriage.

Ben thought about taking the wheel for a while, especially now, with them heading into town, but he decided to leave things as they were. He'd drive after they crossed the river and stopped to refill their water containers. For the time being, he preferred having Sandy behind the wheel so he could be free to defend them from threats. When Joel asked about the Mustang, Ben told him he didn't think they would see it again, but he wasn't sure about that. And as they headed the wrong way down the interstate, Ben couldn't shake the image of running head-on into the old armor-clad Ford and the bike. A part of him, the part that wanted closure on the conflict, wished they would meet again. He hated feeling like he had to keep one eye behind them at all times.

The only good thing about their detour was that the new route would likely throw anyone following them off their trail or at least reduce the odds of being found. In the event the Mustang was still out there, looking for them, the driver would have no way of knowing which way Ben and the others went to continue around the bridge.

Leaving the interstate for a while might be the best move right now. They'd pick it up again a few miles on the other side of Emlenton, but it would be a while before they were back on I-80. The Mustang had been close enough for the driver to see the Colorado plates on the Blazer, so it wouldn't take much to figure out they were headed west and would likely use the interstate to make the best time.

Ben removed his sunglasses and wiped the sweat from his face with a rag. He was over-thinking this and spending too much time worrying about something that might never happen. Maybe the heat was starting to get to him.

"You feeling all right?" Sandy asked.

"Yeah, just can't stop thinking about this morning," Ben confessed.

"Are you worried they might still come after us?"

Ben shrugged. "I don't know. Maybe a little."

"I bet they don't even have their car fixed yet. It looked to be in pretty bad shape," Sandy said.

"You're probably right." He nodded and turned to see if Emma was paying attention to their conversation, but she was still drawing in her notebook.

"There it is. I see the exit up ahead." Sandy took her foot off the gas as they approached. Ben watched the string of vehicles follow the Blazer through a sharp turn onto the ramp. The exit led them onto a small two-lane road that wound its way through the woods for longer than Ben would have expected, based on what he saw on the map.

They passed over a small bridge spanning a steep ravine and a stream of fast-moving water. Ben was tempted to suggest they stop right here for water, but it wasn't ideal. The ravine was too steep and rocky, and the water was a good thirty feet down from the road. From what he could see, the stream looked clean, though, and that was encouraging, but right now, he just wanted to get across the river.

Once they made it through town and were safely on the west side of the Allegheny, he felt like they could relax a little. He'd studied the road atlas well, and as far as he could tell, once they were through here, it was a clear shot to the Ohio border. He couldn't wait to open the map to a new state, anything other than Pennsylvania. They'd had nothing but trouble in this area, starting with the night they tangled with the bears.

In the time it took them to almost get through this state, they had traveled halfway across the country on their trip east. To say it was frustrating was an understatement. He always knew it would take more time because of the northern route they had chosen in order to avoid Pittsburgh, but he never would have imagined it would go like this.

Ben tried to curb his optimism for the time being. There was still no guarantee this bridge would be open, either, and he regretted not taking a look at it through his scope when he had the opportunity. Maybe he would have if he hadn't been in such a hurry to get moving. They'd know for sure in another mile or two.

They had to be close now; they were starting to see the remains of buildings, some burned to the ground, others destroyed by looters. Most of them were houses, but as they rounded the bend onto Main Street, they suddenly found themselves on a very narrow road surrounded by commercial buildings on either side. The exhaust echoed off the building, making it impossible to hear anything but the Blazer. It felt cramped and made Ben uneasy. Some of the shattered storefront windows were less than a few paces away from the truck as they passed by.

Ben slid the KSG across his lap and let it rest partway out the window. So far, they hadn't seen any people, and he was hoping it stayed that way. Maybe the heat was keeping them inside, or maybe there was no one left here. He also noticed that Emma was no longer drawing. Instead, she sat quietly, looking out the window. Even Bajer and Sam were anxious and sitting upright, their ears raised while they searched the passing buildings.

"There's a sign for the interstate. Follow it?" Sandy asked.

"Yeah, that should lead us to the bridge."

Ben saw the sign, too; it looked like a left at the intersection ahead would lead them out of town. He checked on the other vehicles behind them. Joel was bringing up the rear now, something Ben wasn't very happy about. The Scrambler was too far back for his comfort, and the spread between the vehicles was too large.

"Stop at the intersection for a while and let everyone catch up," Ben said.

"Okay." Sandy let the Blazer coast.

"I don't like this place. It's creepy." Emma was slouched down in her seat and leaning toward the middle.

"Try to pick up the pace a little. Over." Ben knew the distance between the vehicles had nothing to do with Joel's driving, but maybe a push from the back would encourage Rita and Martin to speed up.

The Blazer rolled to a stop at the intersection of Main and Kerr Avenue. Straight ahead was a park sign for the Allegheny River Trail, and the road to the right led farther into town. The left was what they wanted, and the bright blue sign that read *I-80 WEST* pointed the way to the bridge and the interstate beyond.

To Ben's immediate left was what was left of the Emlenton fire department. The roof had caved in, but the concrete structure still stood. The trucks were all lined up inside but burned and covered with debris from the collapse. On the right side of the Blazer was a Uni-Mart, a small convenience store and gas station, long ago picked clean by looters. Ben felt a little better now that the rows of buildings lining Main Street so closely had given way to a more open area of town. There was more than just a sidewalk separating them from the broken and battered storefronts, but it was still tight. Although he hated having to stop the Blazer here, if he and Sandy continued around the corner, they would lose sight of the others.

Rita finally caught up to them, and Sandy started to make the turn toward the bridge. Ben leaned forward in his seat, not knowing what to expect but hoping for the best. Once out in the intersection, they could see the bridge clearly. It was less than a half mile away and it looked wide open. A sense of relief washed over him when he laid eyes on the two open lanes. But the feeling didn't last long. When he turned to make sure the others were following, he saw Martin steer the Scout into the Uni-Mart parking lot.

Ben sighed. "What is he doing?"

"We're stopping here?" Emma asked nervously.

"No. I don't know what's going on." The idea that Martin might be having some type of mechanical problem crossed Ben's mind. But when the Scout came to a controlled stop near the underground tank access caps protruding from the asphalt, Ben knew he was out of gas.

"Joel, can you find out what's going on with Martin and get back to me? This isn't a good place to stop. Over."

"Copy that. Over." Ben watched as the Jeep veered off the road and drove over the sidewalk to get next to the Scout. Allie leaned out the window and started talking with Martin. A few seconds passed before the radio crackled to life.

"He's low on fuel. Less than a quarter tank. Over." Ben was furious. Why would he wait until now to mention he needed fuel? He could have said something back at the bridge.

"Great timing. We could have stopped back on the interstate somewhere. We passed at least a dozen places in the last hour alone," Sandy huffed. She was mad, too, and rightfully so. She understood the dangers of fueling up in a place like this. They couldn't see farther than twenty yards in most directions, and in some instances, the buildings blocked their view entirely.

Ben thought for a second. "How's the Jeep on gas? Over."

"We've got just under half a tank. Over," Joel answered.

"Copy that. Sit tight for a second. Over." Ben glanced at the Blazer's fuel gauge and confirmed they had about the same. He was hoping to stop and fill all the vehicles somewhere more remote, like at a standalone gas station off the interstate.

"Pull the truck up enough for Rita to make the turn and get behind us, but don't go past the gas station. I'll be right back." Ben held onto the KSG and slid out of the Blazer. He barely even noticed the pain in his leg as he walked back toward the Toyota and waved Rita forward. She slowed as they passed Ben.

"How much gas do you have?" he asked her.

"Over half a tank."

"Okay, good. I want you guys to go ahead and cross the bridge. Wait for us on the other side, okay?" Ben walked backward a few steps to keep pace with the Toyota while he spoke.

Rita and Carlos both nodded.

"Let them by. They're going to cross over and wait," Ben called out to Sandy, who was leaning out her window and waiting for instructions. He originally thought he wanted the Toyota to at least be in position to roll out quickly if the need arose, but the more he thought about it, the more he liked the idea of them being removed from the equation altogether. If they had to make a hasty exit from town, Rita's driving abilities would slow them down too much.

Ben wasn't sure what was more disappointing: the fact that Martin wasn't communicating with the group and making decisions on his own or that the Scout was an absolute gas hog.

He hadn't expected the fuel economy to be great, but this was ridiculous. Overloading the Scout with ammunition and guns wasn't helping any, and at this rate, they'd have to make twice as many stops. The supped-up International was going to cost them a lot of time.

· 22 ·

Ben started for the Scout but stopped halfway across the narrow two-lane street when he heard a noise.

"What is it?" Allie asked.

"I'm not sure." Ben kept watch down Main Street as he made his way to Martin. "This isn't a good place to stop. How bad are you on gas?"

"I've got a quarter tank, but I just figured since there was a gas station right here—"

Ben cut Martin off before he could finish. "We need to decide things as a group. If you had let us known you were low, we could have topped you off with the jerry cans back at the bridge."

"I wasn't thinking about it then, I guess." Martin hung his head. Ben weighed their options for a moment. He considered putting at least one of the spare cans of fuel into the Scout since they were already stopped, but something about this place wasn't sitting well with him.

"Dad." Joel opened the driver's side door of the Jeep and stood up, looking back toward the section of town they'd just driven through. The expression on his son's face matched the uneasy feeling in his stomach. Ben stepped back from the Scout and saw a small crowd of people moving their way. They were walking slowly but making steady progress toward the vehicles. Some of them had clubs or sections of pipe that had been crudely fashioned into weapons.

One of the men had a sharpened pool cue, stained red with what Ben assumed was blood from another confrontation. The crowd reminded him of the meth-head looters from Falls Creek. Their clothes were tattered and soiled, and most of the group had visible scabs covering their bodies. It was like a scene from a low-budget horror movie, and it took a couple of seconds for Ben to accept what he was seeing was real.

Then a man in the crowd threw an empty bottle their way. The glass shattered on the street, far from reaching them or doing any damage, but it seemed to incite his followers and motivate them to quicken their advance.

"Drive! Go on. Get out of here." Ben made eye contact with Joel as he backed away from the Scout and leveled the KSG at the advancing crowd. There were too many people for him to handle on his own, but he was hoping the shotgun would be enough of a deterrent to at least slow them down. He only needed to buy enough time for Joel and Martin to get out of there.

Joel looked like he wanted to argue but dropped back inside the Jeep and closed the door. He'd been smart and left the Jeep running when they pulled in to check on Martin, and it was only a matter of seconds before he was sitting next to the Blazer and ready to go. The Scout, however, was a different story.

Martin had turned the truck off after pulling in for fuel, and now he was having trouble getting it started again.

"Don't flood it," Ben yelled without looking away from the advancing looters.

Martin threw up his hands. "I'm trying."

The small crowd was growing in size as a few more stragglers joined from the shadows of the abandoned buildings. The mob seemed to be emboldened by the Scout's mechanical trouble, and some of crowd started moving at an ungainly canter toward the gas station. None were carrying guns—none that Ben could see, anyway. But it didn't make the threat any less deadly. The shotgun pointed in their direction seemed to have no effect on their advance. Ben thought about shooting the man he perceived to be the leader of the attack; that usually stopped the other, less-committed participants. But as he glanced back at the Blazer, he saw Emma peeking out from behind the seat.

Ben couldn't shoot a man who was armed with only a stick, not in front of his daughter. Or could he? If Martin couldn't get the truck started, he might not have a choice. Aiming high, he unleashed one of the Dragon's Breath rounds into the air above the mob. The magnesium-fueled fireball lit up the street above the crowd, stopping the looters in their tracks for a moment. Remnants of white-hot magnesium rained down on them in a shower of sparks. A few scattered, seeking shelter in the burnt-out storefronts.

Ben was disappointed to see that most remained and collected themselves quickly to resume their advance. These were people who had nothing left to live for. Based on the looks on some of their faces, Ben thought they might rather be put out of their misery by a bullet than suffer another day of this post-apocalyptic hell.

Ben flicked the lever and switched over to the barrel holding the double-aught buckshot. For the first time in his life, he hoped for a large spread on the steel shot, and with any luck, he'd be able to take out a couple of the looters with a single shell. He hated doing this while Emma and Brad had a front-row seat, but they were running out of time.

"Come on, you stupid..."

Bang!

The Scout roared to life with an explosive backfire and a large puff of black smoke from the exhaust before Martin could finish screaming at it.

"Go!" Ben yelled while backpedaling toward the Blazer. "Everybody, go!"

Joel pulled out first in the Jeep and headed for the bridge. The Scout lurched forward when Martin threw it into gear and began moving out. But not before losing the rear window to a chunk of concrete thrown from the crowd. Several looters had made it to within reach of the fleeing Scout, and one of them lunged for the opening left by the broken window. The man caught the truck with one hand, but the broken glass cut into his palm and he let go after only being dragged a couple of feet. Landing on the pavement face-down, he was trampled by the others as they continued the chase.

Sandy had the Blazer rolling and the passenger door open for Ben while he sprinted the rest of the way.

"Go, go, go." He threw the KSG into the truck, then grabbed the door and pulled himself inside. Before he had a chance to close it, Sandy stomped on the gas, pinning him to the back of his seat. By the time he was able to sit up and take stock of what had happened, the mob had dwindled to a few die-hards still chasing them but falling away fast as they sped off. They were nearly caught up to the Scout, which was now halfway across the bridge. Ben and

Emma continued watching, along with Sam and Bajer, as the rest of the assailants gave up the chase and resorted to waving sticks at them.

Sandy had a tight grip on the steering wheel and was still picking up speed.

"It's over. We're safe. You can slow down now," Ben urged. Her face was as white as her knuckles, and the biggest threat now was her getting into an accident.

"What was that? They... They were like animals. I've never seen anything like that in my life," Sandy said through labored breathing while continually checking her mirror.

Ben was glad to see her slowing down. He checked behind them once more to satisfy himself and confirm it was truly over. He noticed Emma still watching as the bridge slipped out of sight.

"Let's go at least five miles before we pull over and regroup. Over," Ben said into the radio. He then swapped it for a Nalgene bottle and forced down some warm water.

"Copy that. Over," Joel answered.

"That was desperation. And I'm afraid we're going to see a lot more of it." It was a truth Sandy and Emma needed to hear and understand. The next time they found themselves in a similar situation, they might not be so lucky. He might have to shoot someone whose only weapon was a stick or a rock. It didn't mean they were any less dangerous, and everyone needed to recognize that. It wasn't the weapon that made a person dangerous; it was their state of mind. And those people back there wouldn't have hesitated to kill them all for one of their MREs.

Ben's fears were being realized. He'd always anticipated things taking a turn for the worse, but what they had just experienced was undeniable proof it was happening now. He thought it would take longer for people to abandon their sense of civility. Maybe the radiation had affected their brains as well. Judging by the scabs, blisters, and missing hair, Ben had no doubt they'd been exposed to high levels of it.

The proximity to Pittsburgh and the lower-altitude detonation of the EMP that destroyed the city were also factors, he thought. Did that mean this was what they should expect from now on when passing through an area that had been hit hard or was close to ground zero for one of the nukes? On the other hand, this couldn't go on for long.

People like the ones they had just escaped would start to die off. He wasn't sure what the life expectancy was for someone with extreme radiation poisoning, but he didn't think it could be long, based on the way they looked. It was a morbid thought, one that made him feel slightly guilty, but he hoped they would die off soon, especially if that was the type of reception they could expect everywhere they stopped.

· 23 ·

Not much was said over the next few miles. Ben hated to admit it, but he was bothered more than he should have been by the incident back in town, and he knew the others were as well. It wasn't the first close call they'd had by any stretch of the imagination, but it was different than any of the other encounters they'd had thus far. There was something strange about the people who had attacked them. There was a look in their eye he couldn't explain. The expressions on their faces reminded him of a trapped, panicked animal fighting for its life. But there was something more to it, something else, that made them seem almost inhuman.

Any unprepared survivors, like the mob in town, should be weak and emaciated without proper supplies, yet the majority had the strength to run, throw heavy objects, and swing pipes and two-by-fours over their heads. Maybe adrenaline and the chance to steal some food had enabled their strength. Whatever the case, he didn't want to think about it anymore and tried to put it out of his mind.

After about ten minutes or so of driving, Joel pulled off the highway and onto a narrow dirt road that led them back toward the river. A few more miles of potholes and tree branches scraping down the side of the truck and they found themselves staring at the Allegheny River. Its muddy waters weren't exactly what Ben had hoped for, but other than the sediment, it looked free of any chemicals or man-made pollutants. He was also pleased that this was an isolated spot; he couldn't see any signs of Emlenton from here.

He wasn't worried about the people who had chased them through town. They were all on foot, and he was sure they'd given up as soon as they were out of sight. And for the first time in a while, he had zero concerns that the Mustang would find them here. It would be another couple of miles before the road they'd been traveling on would connect with the interstate. If it weren't so early in the day, this would have made a great spot to spend the night. But he had more ambitious plans for them today.

Thanks to the river, the trees lining its banks retained their lush foliage and provided some much-needed shade from the intense early-afternoon sun. Initially, Ben's intentions were to only stay here long enough to replenish their depleted water supply. But now that they were here, and he was comfortable with the security of the location, he was okay with staying longer. They'd put in a hard half day of driving, and it would do them a world of good to sit still in the shade for a short time and have something to eat.

Of course, he'd wanted to be farther along by now; they hadn't come close to reaching the progress he'd hoped for. They definitely made better time when it was just the Blazer and the Jeep, but that was a played-out argument he didn't want taking up any more space in his head.

"It doesn't feel half bad here in the shade." Allie got out of the Jeep and stood motionless for a second, enjoying the shade and basking in the slight breeze coming in off the river. Gunner jumped down from the open door and bolted for the water. Wasting no time, he was belly-deep in seconds and taking in sloppy mouthfuls of the brown liquid. Sam and Bajer watched anxiously from the Blazer, whining and waiting for their chance to escape the confines of the vehicle. As soon as Sandy parked, Ben jumped out and stepped back so as to not get run over by the two exuberant dogs. Sam joined Gunner without hesitation, but Bajer was more reserved and stayed closer to the shoreline. She was equally enthusiastic about the opportunity to play in the water but seemed satisfied to run along the bank in the shallows.

No one tried to stop the dogs from swimming or playing in the water this time. Riding with wet dogs didn't seem like such a big deal in comparison to all they had been through today. At least that was how Ben felt. He didn't blame the dogs; it would have felt great to take a quick dip, but he didn't have the energy or want to take the time to clean up after.

"Should we have a meal here?" Sandy asked.

Ben nodded. "That's what I was thinking."

The fresh air blowing in off the water did feel good, and for a few moments, Ben forgot how mad he was at Martin for putting them all at risk and pulling a stunt like that back in town.

Martin approached Ben at the water's edge. "Sorry about stopping back there. I didn't think it would be that big of a deal to stop and I saw the gas station right there, so...so I just thought it would save us some time."

Standing there in the shade and listening to the water rush by had squelched Ben's desire to lay into Martin about what happened. And at this point, he didn't even want to talk about it, let alone argue. "It was a hard lesson learned. We need to communicate better, that's all. We never stop in places that congested, and now you know why."

Ben remained focused on the far side of the river as he spoke. He feared that looking at the guy might rekindle his frustration about the incident.

"Yeah, it was a stupid thing to do," Martin agreed.

Ben inhaled the fresh air deeply and blew it out through his nose. It was time to move on. Martin seemed genuine in his apology, and dwelling on it any longer wouldn't accomplish anything. The lesson had been learned.

"Why don't you grab the jerry cans and empty them both into your truck? That should give you about half a tank. Should be enough to get you to the next fuel stop." Ben turned to look at Martin this time.

"Yeah, I'll do that right now." Martin headed for the vehicles.

Joel and Allie were already busy unloading the empty water containers and filter. Brad and Emma helped carry the containers down to the water's edge.

"Come on, guys. Let's set up out there by those rocks, away from the dogs." Joel pointed to a cluster of smooth rocks protruding above the surface and isolating a small section of the river from the faster-moving water. The kids took off their shoes and started to wade out to the spot in knee-deep water. Ben thought about recommending that they filter water from somewhere that didn't require them to take off their shoes, but he decided not to.

"Oh, that feels so good." Emma stood in water up to her shins and wiggled her feet in the mud. The dogs saw that the kids were in now and headed over to join them.

"No, stay." Joel held up his hand. "Em, that's your job, okay? Keep the dogs out of this area. If they stir up a bunch of mud, it'll take twice as long to get this done."

"Okay," Emma happily agreed. She searched the bank and found a stick to keep the dogs occupied while the others got to work pumping water through the filter. Rita was helping Sandy prepare a meal consisting of something other than MREs for a change, and Ben was happy to see that.

Joel took a break from pumping the filter handle and looked out across the water. "Maybe we could catch some fish here."

"Maybe, but water first," Ben answered. It would be nice to have some protein that didn't come out of a pouch for a change, but Ben wasn't sure if they had enough time or if anything could be caught here. If they finished refilling the water containers first, there wouldn't be any harm in letting Joel try. Whatever they could catch, or hunt, would be their only source of fresh meat now. Thanks to the moonshiners, they had no venison left. Then again, with this heat, the deer meat would have expired long ago anyway.

Ben wandered over to the Toyota, where Carlos was sitting on the tailgate. "How are you feeling?"

"Better, thanks. Starting to get my strength back. I still get a little dizzy when I stand up, though."

"Well, just take it easy. You'll get there." Ben hoped that was the case so Rita could take a break from driving. The thought of putting Allie behind the wheel of the Toyota crossed his mind again, but that was something he would only consider as a last resort. He still didn't like the idea of splitting up the kids. Hopefully this little pit stop would give Rita a chance to rest up enough to finish the day strong. Ben still had every intention of reaching Ohio tonight before stopping to make camp.

But this was too nice of a spot to think about leaving right now. Ben found a large flat rock by the water and leaned his rifle against it before sitting down to watch the kids for a minute. They were all busy taking turns pumping the filter handle and laughing about something. Seeing them carrying on and splashing water on one another made Ben smile. They were finally occupied with something other than running for their lives. They'd been doing that a lot lately, or so it seemed. It was the first time he'd seen Emma smile today. Not that there had been much to smile about, but she'd been a little off since they left the motel, and her mood had gone downhill ever since.

Ben tried to put himself in her shoes and imagine how the world looked to her. The early teenage years were tough enough without having to see the things she'd seen over the last couple of weeks. He was lucky she was talking at all, and seeing her fool around with the other kids made him think he was expecting too much from her.

In times like these, he also appreciated having Sandy and Allie with them. He could only imagine how hard it would be for Emma if she were surrounded by boys through all this. Allie and Sandy were both great role models, and he was grateful for that. Not once did Ben have to ask twice when there was work to be done. In fact, there were times when he felt like nothing needed to be said at all. They'd been traveling together now for almost two weeks, and most of the time, everyone knew their role.

Ben glanced back to check on Martin and his progress with the jerry cans. He thought about offering the guy a hand. He felt guilty watching him work, but not enough to move from the rock he was sitting on.

Ben turned his attention to Sandy and Rita making lunch over the tailgate of the Toyota and realized he'd been sitting there longer than he intended.

"I'm sorry. Do you guys need any help?" Ben called over to the ladies.

"Nope, we got it. I'll let you do the dishes, though." Sandy shot him a smile.

"What are you guys making? It smells great," Martin chimed in.

"Just rice and veggies," Rita answered.

"I guess I'm just hungry." Martin went back to pouring the last can of fuel into the Scout.

If no one needed his help with anything, Ben wasn't going to let this opportunity go to waste, so he slipped off his boots and socks. The water felt better than it looked, and he enjoyed the coolness of it as he buried his feet in the sandy mud of the riverbank. It would have been easy to call it a day right here and now, but it would be a decision they would regret come morning, when they found themselves still in Pennsylvania. Besides, he'd promised to put this part of the map behind them and had assured the others they'd see Ohio tonight.

· 24 ·

As hungry as Ben was and as good as the food smelled, he wished it had taken a little longer to prepare. He was enjoying the water on his feet, and for the first time in a while, he wasn't sweating. It didn't take much convincing to talk Sandy into joining him on the rock for lunch. She went barefoot as well and splashed her feet in the water alongside him as they ate.

Ben wasn't sure why, but he felt safe here. They were far off the road and there were no signs of life in any direction, but it was more than that. Maybe it was because he felt like they had been under attack, or at least the threat of it, all day.

The kids had quieted down after lunch and the dogs were sleeping under a nearby tree after filling their bellies with dog food and all the river water they could drink. Joel had either forgotten about fishing or fallen victim to post-lunch laziness, although Ben suspected his lack of enthusiasm about pursuing fish had more to do with the fact that Allie was resting her head on his shoulder and holding his hand. Ben tried not to stare at the young couple, but it felt good to see them living their lives in spite of all this going on around them. It gave him hope that life would return to normal someday.

"Well, I hate to say it, but..." Ben sighed.

"Oh, I know, I know." Sandy arched her back and stretched. "Back behind the wheel."

"I was thinking I'd drive for a while and give you a break. You've done more than your share today and I appreciate it."

"Are you sure you feel up to it?" Sandy frowned. "I see the way you've been holding your side."

"It won't hurt any more in the driver's seat than it does now. Besides, if I stare at the map any more, I might go insane. I know every exit from here to Cloverdale by heart." Ben laughed.

"Okay, if you say so. By the way, how much farther are we going today? I know you said Ohio, but how many more hours of driving do you think it'll take?"

"Hard to say, not knowing what kind of speed we can maintain or what we'll run into, but barring anything major, I'm hoping to get where we need to be in about four or five hours if we can get away with just one more fuel stop," Ben added before sliding over to the side of the rock that faced dry ground.

"That's not too bad. Do you have a place in mind?" Sandy moved to his other side and pushed her feet out into a thin sliver of sunlight on the grass.

"There's a creek called Little Yankee Run just over the border into Ohio. That's what we're shooting for. The creek shares its headwaters with this river, so it should be good, clean water. Maybe the boys can catch us a few fish for dinner."

"That would be nice. The motel was comfortable last night, but I think I actually prefer camping... without the bears." Sandy wrinkled her brow.

Ben tilted his head. "I've spent my fair share of time sleeping outdoors, and I can tell you that was a first for me as well. I wouldn't let it bother you. It will probably never happen again."

"Probably? You said 'probably.'" She smiled this time and stood up.

Ben joined her but remained silent, only grinning as he headed for the truck.

"I saw that," Sandy joked.

"Hey, are you guys finished filtering water?" Ben called out to the kids, changing the subject on purpose.

"Yeah, everything's loaded up except the bottles everyone has on them," Allie answered.

"Sounds good. What do you say we aim to be back on the road in five?" Ben asked.

"Okay," Joel said while the others nodded in agreement. Ben checked in with Rita and Carlos to make sure they were on board with the schedule, and they were. He met Martin around the backside of the Blazer and helped him secure the empty jerry cans to the truck. Ben figured they had a good hour or so before anyone's fuel would reach a critical level.

The Scout's poor gas mileage was definitely going to be more of an issue than he'd originally feared. Planning their stops would be crucial to their safety, something he hoped Martin was well aware of now. Ben wished they had a couple more spare cans to fill; at this rate, the Scout was probably going to cost them two extra stops a day. He was beginning to regret the idea of taking the extra arms and supplies to Cloverdale and wondered if the plan was a foolish one. He might have abandoned the whole thing if he didn't feel like he was indebted to the Major and some of the other townsfolk there.

Without the sanctuary they found in Cloverdale, they might very well still be on their way to Maryland. That was nothing short of reality, and Ben knew it. He was also fully aware that if they hadn't reached Jack's when they did, it would have been too late for Emma and Brad's sake.

Between the Blazer's mechanical issues and Gunner's injuries, they were in bad shape, and without the help they found in Cloverdale, things would be quite different today.

Ben thought the supplies were the least they could do for the town, especially if they were going to crash there again for at least a night. And he was sure Vince would be more than happy to top off their tanks and put them all up for the night once he saw what was in the back of the Scout. But Cloverdale was important for other reasons, primarily since it was a place willing to help people in need, and that was rare these days.

A cache of weapons and ammo, the likes of which were in the back of the Scout, could carry a town like that for an awfully long time if it was conserved. That might be easier said than done, though, with nightly attacks from the gang of looters that seemed intent on taking over the town and seizing its supplies. One or the other would give in sooner or later. Ben hoped it wasn't Vince and his people. Actually, he was counting on it, as much as he hated to admit that. If things kept unfolding the way they were out here on the road, Ben and the others would need Cloverdale as badly as Cloverdale needed the resupply of weapons and ammunition.

Everyone started to load into the vehicles. Emma and Allie did their best to clean the dogs up with towels before coaxing them into the trucks. Sam was showing her age and needed to be lifted into the Blazer. After all the running and swimming they had done, the dogs were moving a little slow. Except Bajer, who flew up into the passenger seat and made her way to the back of the truck with little effort. Even Gunner needed a boost and was only willing to exert enough energy to place his front paws up on the doorsill, where he waited for Joel to pick up his rear end and push him the rest of the way into the Jeep. It was a lazy habit Ben had seen before after a long day of duck-hunting.

With everyone ready to leave, he thought it would be a good idea to give them all a short rundown on the afternoon's plan, or at least what he was shooting for. He especially wanted to be clear with Martin on when and where they would stop next. He didn't need any more surprises today. Admittedly, that was something they couldn't control, but reining Martin in would certainly reduce the chances of things going south. Ben thought for a moment about what he was going to say. He'd try his best to make it sound like he wasn't picking on the guy.

"All right, I hope that was a good recharge for you all. I just wanted to go over the plan for the afternoon with everyone before heading out." He scanned the small group of people surrounding him.

It was hard to believe that what started out as him and Joel driving to Maryland had turned into a group of nine heading west. Some of the faces belonged to complete strangers less than a few days ago. And now these people were entrusting their lives to him. It was not a responsibility he asked for, but it was one that he took seriously.

"So what's the plan?" Joel asked.

"The plan is to camp in Ohio tonight on the Little Yankee Run. It's a medium-sized creek that looks to be about an hour's drive from the border. If we can keep the stops to a minimum, I think we'll arrive with some daylight remaining. I was thinking you boys could catch us some fresh trout for dinner." Ben watched as Joel and Brad looked at each other and smiled.

"How long do you think it will take overall to get there?" Rita asked.

"My best guess is around four or five hours." Ben opened the map and laid it across the hood of the Blazer. "We're right about here. I'm hoping to get here."

Rita stepped forward as he pointed to Little Yankee Run. She glanced back at her husband with a concerned look on her face. Ben knew it was a lot to ask of her.

"We'll break it up. We have no choice, really, because of the Scout. Based on the fuel Martin went through today, I'd say with the ten gallons he just added, we've got about an hour and a half of driving before he needs to stop." Ben looked at Martin, then at the Scout.

Martin shrugged. "I'm trying to take it easy, but it doesn't seem to matter."

"I know. You're doing a good job driving. The fuel economy might improve when we reach flat land, but not by much. We can deal with stopping for gas, though. We've got the equipment to get in and out pretty fast. It's the unplanned or impulsive stops that hurt us." Ben remained focused on Martin as he spoke.

"It would be easier with another radio," Martin argued.

"You're right, but we don't have one, so you need to use the hand signals Allie wrote down for you. And use them early, not the moment you realize you're on empty." The calmness Ben had felt near the river was beginning to slip away.

Martin threw up his hands. "I lost the paper. I was afraid I was going to give the wrong signal."

"Then we'll get you another copy. We've come too far and worked too hard to make stupid mistakes," Ben shot back.

"Well, I've only been with you for a couple days, and I'm not very good at all this." Martin was pacing back and forth now. Ben felt someone's hand on his shoulder and turned to see Sandy. He took a deep breath and paused for a moment.

She was right; arguing was a waste of time and energy, and it wasn't getting them any closer to Cloverdale.

"We just need to work as a team. The stakes are too high and there's no second chances. I'm sorry I yelled. I just want us all to be safe." Ben had already said more than he intended to; he certainly didn't plan on getting into it with Martin like that. But maybe it was best to get everything out in the open. He'd been holding some of that in since this morning, and the snafu back in town had nearly pushed him over the edge. But the thing that bothered him most was that, prior to today's events, he was just starting to think Martin was catching on to the way they did things.

"This is all crazy. Are we insane? I mean, where are we going, anyway? I don't even have a home anymore. Why don't you just leave me here to die?" Martin started pacing again and biting his nails. He was spiraling out of control, and it was starting to freak out the kids. The last thing they needed was a grown man having a nervous breakdown right here in front of them. But mostly, Ben couldn't help but feel a little guilty about the fact that he was more concerned with the time it would cost them.

He approached Martin mid-stride and stepped into his path. Looking him straight in the eye, Ben grabbed both of his shoulders and held him in place at arm's length.

"Nobody is leaving you here to die, you hear me? And your home is with us—or in Cloverdale or wherever you choose it to be. Take a drink of water and get a grip." Ben had meant that to come out better than it sounded, and he doubted it did much to ease Martin's nerves, which was why he was more than willing to step out of the way and let Sandy have a crack at smoothing things over. He didn't have the patience for this today.

"Look, Martin, I know you've been through a lot—we all have—but we need to stick together. There's strength in numbers, and that's what we have here: strength. But we need you to stay with us, okay? We're a team, right?" Sandy looked around at the others, who had picked up on her cue and chimed in with encouraging words of their own. Ben stayed silent, afraid he would let slip something worse than what he'd already said.

Martin did seem to come to his senses a little after Sandy's pep talk, but Ben had one eye on his watch, and he was growing impatient. As soon as he saw the opportunity to speed things along, he spoke up.

"Everybody good to go? The longer we spend here, the longer we'll be on the road tonight." Ben only made brief eye contact with Martin this time.

"Yeah, we're ready. Let's go. I want to get there before it gets dark." Joel headed for the Jeep with Allie and Brad right behind him.

"Hang in there, Martin. This is your second chance at life. At least we're not still trapped in those containers, right? It can always be worse." Carlos did his best to encourage Martin while Rita laid a hand on his back before they both started for the Toyota.

"We'll do our best not to slow you all down," Rita called out to everyone.

"Joel, you stay in the lead. We'll keep bringing up the rear. Everybody in the same order that we've been in," Ben shouted before climbing into the Blazer. Emma hopped up into the truck and joined the dogs on the back seat. While Ben waited for Sandy to get in, he watched Allie run what he assumed was another copy of the hand signals over to Martin. Then she returned to the Jeep.

"Oh, good, I was going to do that. At least he has them now." Sandy buckled herself in.

"Yeah, let's hope he remembers to use them." Ben waited until it was their turn to pull out and gave the Scout plenty of room ahead of them. It felt good to be behind the wheel again, and other than the argument with Martin, the stop had been a good one. He reached his hand back and patted Emma's leg. She returned his affection with a brief smile in the rearview mirror and then went back to insulating the water bottles with towels while the dogs made their spots awkwardly around her.

Ben had high hopes for the remainder of the afternoon, and he had every right to, didn't he? Hadn't they been through enough for one day already? They deserved a break. Things couldn't keep going like this the rest of the way to Colorado.

Or could they?

· 25 ·

It wasn't long before they found blacktop again and were headed west on a small two-lane road lined with half-dead trees. The landscape away from the river wasn't much to look at, but the familiar hum of the tires was music to Ben's ears. And for once, he was feeling optimistic about reaching Ohio tonight. They were more than halfway there, and even with the fuel stops factored in, they should make it to the campsite long before dark.

The sense of accomplishment didn't last long, though, and he started wondering if they shouldn't be pushing farther tonight. He tried to dismiss the thought, reminding himself how important it was to take their time and be selective about where they stopped. Just because the place looked like it had potential on the map didn't mean it would turn out to be a suitable or safe place to spend the night. Better to take their time finding the right spot before committing to setting up camp, then waking up to find out they'd made a mistake. And that could require driving farther than expected.

There were no guarantees anymore. The creek on the map could be polluted or, in this heat, bone dry. Ben pictured the oily sheen swirling on the surface of the stream they crossed while traveling east. That was one of the spots he marked on the map to avoid on their way home. And it was another area of the country that wouldn't improve with this weather, although the storm last night gave him hope. Depending on what they found tonight, it might be best to ration their water. After they'd gone through so much water at the motel yesterday and this morning, he'd be sure to keep a closer eye on their usage going forward.

But that was one of the advantages of camping, as far as he was concerned. He could see what was going on and what everyone was doing. He wasn't worried about his kids wasting resources; they knew the drill when camping and understood you couldn't operate the spicket on the water jug like you ran the tap at home. Allie and her mom were equally competent at this point and appreciated the scarceness of supplies. But he wasn't so sure about the others. With everyone in separate rooms last night, he had no idea where so much of the water had gone. He had his suspicions but didn't want to point another finger at Martin. Not yet, anyway, even though he did look rather well-groomed this morning, all things considered.

Ben didn't want to think about Martin right now, though. It was bad enough he had to stare at the back of the Scout, a constant reminder they were going to have to stop again and get gas. Most of the trouble they ran into was the result of an unlucky fuel stop. But thirsty Scout or not, it was a necessary evil.

They'd been on the road for one hour and forty-five minutes exactly. Ben knew because he was watching the time and waiting for Martin's arm to pop out of the window and signal that he needed to stop. The last readable sign they'd passed said it was thirty-nine miles to Hubbard, Ohio. They were just a few miles from the border now, making it all the more bothersome that they were going to have to stop soon. Ben was hoping they could at least make it out of the state before doing that. He couldn't blame the Scout this time, though. The Blazer was nearing a quarter tank, and he knew the Jeep was probably running at about the same.

"We're getting close, huh?" Sandy had the atlas on her lap.

"Very. It would be nice to get out of PA before we stop. I've seen enough of it to last me a lifetime."

"How are we on gas?" Sandy leaned over. "Oh, I see."

"Yeah, I'm afraid it's about that time." Ben stuck his arm out the window and began signaling Martin. Like it or not, they needed to find a place to fuel up. With both jerry cans emptied into the Scout, they were without a safety net in the fuel department. Might as well start the process of scouting for a place. Martin finally waved back. Ben tapped the door a few times and followed it up with three sets of five fingers to indicate they should find a place in the next fifteen minutes or so. Martin gave a thumbs-up, but Ben wondered if he'd picked up on the fifteen-minutes bit.

It was time to let Joel know what the plan was over the radio, but Ben wanted Sandy to do it.

"You want to let the kids know?" He handed her the radio.

"Sure." Sandy pressed the mic and the radio squealed. "What am I doing wrong?" she yanked it away from her face.

"That's funny. They must be trying to get ahold of us at the same…" Ben's voice trailed off.

"What is it?" Sandy followed his gaze out the window and saw the large red and blue sign for herself.

OHIO WELCOMES YOU. But it wasn't the friendly greeting that had Ben's attention. The skull and cross-bones painted over the sign had him concerned. Large streaks of black paint ran from the graffiti, and he almost missed the letters written out below.

PH TERRITORY. The writing was sloppy, and he read it again to himself to make sure.

"PH territory?" Sandy shook her head. "What does that mean?"

"No idea, but it doesn't look like they want company," Ben answered. Great, just what they needed, and only because they had to stop soon. He didn't know what, or who, the PH was, but they could have this place. Ben would happily pass through and leave this area to them if he could. But that wasn't an option.

Joel's voice crackled over the radio in Sandy's hand. "Come in, Dad. Over."

"Here." She shoved the radio at Ben.

"Go ahead. Over."

"Did you guys see that? Over," Joel asked.

"Yes. Over." Ben didn't know what else to say about it.

"What are we going to do? I'm gonna need gas soon. Over," Joel said.

"We all do, unfortunately. Keep looking for a place to stop. Over." Ben thought about the sign and its possible meaning. The graffiti could be old. Maybe the people responsible for it weren't even around anymore. But he had no way of knowing, not that it would have mattered anyway. With both jerry cans empty, it wasn't a matter of *if* they would stop, but *when*. They would have to do their best to pick a place that looked the least dangerous, however they were supposed to do that.

Now he wished they'd fueled up sooner. They had passed plenty of gas stations in the last half hour or so, but Ben had been so determined to put Pennsylvania behind them that he avoided stopping until they absolutely had to.

"I see a place up ahead. Over," Joel announced.

"What's it look like? Over." Ben leaned toward Sandy in an attempt to see past the Scout, but he couldn't. "Can you see what he's talking about?" he asked her.

"Not yet." Sandy strained to look ahead, but Martin was already slowing down, and Ben did the same.

Joel's voice came back over the radio. "It looks like all the others. At least it's close to the road. Over."

"I see it." Sandy pointed.

"Okay, you guys know the drill. Be ready for anything, and if something doesn't look right or feel right, get out of there. We'll find another spot. The trucks have a few more miles left in them. Over," Ben warned Joel.

"Copy that. Over."

Ben set the radio down and put both hands on the wheel. He glanced back to let Emma know they were stopping but she was sleeping again.

"I wish I could sleep that easy," Sandy joked.

Ben shook his head. "Yeah, must be nice."

"Should I wake her?"

"Let her sleep. We're not gonna be here long anyway. I wanted to try doing this without even letting the dogs out if we can help it." Ben was going to do his best to make this the quickest refueling stop yet.

"What do you need me to do?" Sandy asked.

"Joel and Martin can help me pump gas. I need the rest of you to keep a lookout. If there's anybody around here, we need to be ready. Keep your AR on you at all times here." Ben probably didn't need to remind her to carry her weapon, but he wasn't leaving anything to chance. If he was going to try and be fast, he wouldn't be able to keep an eye out for trouble very well. That responsibility would fall on the others.

Ben could see the place clearly now. The Loves gas station sign towered above the interstate from a cluster of trees just off the exit. The sign was in good shape, only missing the bright LEDs that normally advertised the price per gallon to highway travelers. It towered over a large service center that primarily catered to eighteen-wheelers, but there was a set of pumps off to one side for cars as well. The convenience store and small restaurant advertised on the sign were no longer standing. But the oversized parking lot made it easy to see down the interstate in both directions and gave them plenty of room to maneuver, should the need arise.

Ben wasn't crazy about the secondary road that ran past the place and made a sudden turn before disappearing around a corner.

The Blazer brought up the rear as the line of vehicles snaked its way around the perimeter of the property.

"It looks good to me. Over," Joel said over the radio.

"It'll have to do. Find the tanks and let's get this done." Ben watched the Jeep veer off to the corner of the lot and stop. Everyone else pulled in next to the Scrambler and parked close together. Ben was the last one stopped but almost the first one out of the truck. He didn't waste any time and started breaking out the hose and pump. "Grab those jerry cans. We might as well fill those too."

Martin had just hopped down from the truck and was mid-stretch. "What about that sign, huh? What do you make of it?"

"It's just a scare tactic to keep people away. I'm not worried about it too much, but I also don't want to linger here any longer than necessary. No reason to push our luck." Ben spoke without looking away from the pump.

"I agree." Martin started untying the jerry cans from the Blazer.

"Hey, Joel, make sure it's not a diesel tank," Ben called out to his son, who was inspecting the fill valves sticking out of the blacktop.

"They're not marked. I'm not sure." Joel stood over the row of metal lids.

"Get one open and we'll find out." Ben ran over to his son with a length of hose ready to push into the tank. Joel pulled one of the caps off and stepped aside while his dad ran the hose down the tube and brought it back out after it touched the bottom. He took a few long strides away from the tanks and dumped some of the freshly extracted fuel onto the ground. "I need a lighter."

Ben barely had the words out when Sandy tossed him one from the truck. He held the flame to the small puddle of liquid and waited. Nothing.

He looked at Joel. "No good. Try another."

Joel had another cap off in a matter of seconds, and Ben plunged the hose into the ground once again. He knew they'd found gasoline this time around even before lighting the puddle on fire, based on how quickly it was evaporating off the hot asphalt.

"Good to go. Let's start filling the tanks." Ben gave the order, and Joel and Martin sprang into action. They moved as fast as they could and didn't stop until every vehicle and jerry can was topped off. They would have normally taken a few breaks in this type of heat, but that was a luxury they could not afford right now. Martin redeemed himself a little in Ben's eyes by hustling through the job without complaint. Martin was a big help, and his and Joel's efforts allowed Ben to keep half an eye out for any unwanted visitors.

The lack of air moving through the Blazer had woken Emma from her nap, and before Ben realized what was happening, Sam and Bajer were running around the parking lot. Gunner, determined not to be left out, leaped from the back of the Jeep and ran to catch up with them.

"Gunner, no," Brad yelled, but it was too late. Gunner ignored the command and disappeared behind the side of the half-destroyed building with the other dogs.

"Gunner, come here," Ben called after the dog this time, but Gunner did not return.

"You guys finish up. I'll go get them." Ben started for the building.

"Want me to help?" Allie offered.

"No, that's okay. I'd rather you stay here and watch the road. Thanks, though." Ben made his way to the burned-out structure as fast as his knee would allow and found the dogs sniffing around a dumpster at the backside of the building.

"Come on, guys. Let's go." Ben fussed at all three of them, but they paid him no mind. He thought about the raccoon chase Gunner led them on a while ago. He really needed to get them away from the dumpster before this took a turn for the worse. They didn't have time to waste. He was about to turn and walk away in an effort to motivate the dogs but stopped. There, on the wall in front of him, the letters *PH* were scratched onto the concrete. Ben didn't need any more reasons to leave, but this was a good one.

"Hey...come on... Let's go—now!" It wasn't until he raised his voice that the dogs acknowledged his presence. Bajer was the first to abandon the scent trail, followed by Gunner, who recognized Ben's tone and knew better than to ignore it. Sam was reluctant to give in so easily, though, and it took a light swat on the rump to get her moving back toward the truck. Ben rolled his eyes. He still found it hard to believe that they had ended up with three large dogs to care for.

"Come on, guys. This isn't the place for exploring. We'll make it up to you later." Ben spoke to the dogs as if they understood what he was saying. He felt bad for them. They had been couped up in the trucks for the last couple of hours along with everyone else. He wished they all could have taken a short breather here, but it wasn't worth the risk.

When Ben returned with the dogs, Joel and Martin had the jerry cans tied down and were ready to get underway.

"Come on, boy." Brad stuck his arm over the side of the Jeep and smacked his hand on the sheet metal. This time, Gunner listened. Emma was waiting by the Blazer and coaxed Sam and Bajer back into the truck, then climbed in herself. They were ready to go, and Ben was amazed to see that less than half an hour had passed since they pulled off the interstate. That was a record for sure, but not one he wanted to try and repeat at this time of day again. They were all soaked with sweat. The remainder of the drive today would be uncomfortable at best.

"You hear that?" Allie stood up on the doorsill of the Jeep with her hand to her ear.

Ben stopped in his tracks and listened. He didn't hear anything at first, but slowly, the rumble of distant exhaust pipes grew louder. He couldn't tell which direction it was coming from. The interstate was clear in both directions, but one thing was certain: it was headed their way.

· 26 ·

"Move the trucks around back. Quick." Ben jumped into the Blazer and fired it up. He threw the truck into gear and started pulling out before Sandy could get her door closed all the way. Joel and Martin were quick to get the Jeep and Scout rolling, but Rita seemed to be moving in slow motion.

There wasn't much left of the old truck stop, but the rear wall of the building was still intact. Whether it was big enough to hide all four vehicles from the road remained to be seen, but it was better than sitting out here in the open. Ben stopped the truck abruptly once they were hidden and jumped out, directing the others to pull in next to the Blazer as close as they could.

Rita was last in line and had barely made it around the corner when a bright red Chevy with two flags mounted to the back bumper appeared on the secondary road that ran past the truck stop.

The big red pickup had come from around the blind corner Ben had concerns about when they first arrived. Good thing Allie heard the truck approaching. The jacked-up Chevy's straight pipes had given it away and afforded them an opportunity to hide.

Ben and the others gathered at the corner of the building and watched the truck slow down before coming to a stop at the intersection of the east- and westbound exits for the interstate. No one said a word while they waited for the truck to move on.

"Do you think they saw us?" Allie asked.

"I don't think so. Just sit tight for a minute and let's see what they do." Ben hoped he was right. It was hard to say if the truck had spotted the Toyota or not, but he didn't think so. If they'd been seen, the Chevy would have pulled into the gas station for sure.

"There they go," Sandy said.

"That figures. They had to go west, didn't they?" Martin sighed loudly. Ben was glad to see the truck move on, but he would have felt a whole lot better if they'd gone the other direction. He watched as the Chevy accelerated up the ramp toward the freeway and saw something that gave him chills. The two flags being flown from the rear bumper straightened in the wind and unfurled, revealing the same skull and crossbones they'd seen painted on the sign a few miles back.

The other was filled with bright red letters that read, *PATRIOT HOOLIGANS*.

"PH. That makes sense," Allie said quietly.

"You noticed that, too, huh?" Ben stepped back from the corner of the building.

"I guess they are still around here," Sandy said.

"Yep. And I'm willing to bet there's a lot more than just the one truck around here." Ben wasn't sure what they should do. At the very least, they needed to give the Chevy a few minutes to move down the interstate.

"Are we still going to go that way?" Joel peeked around the corner again.

"We still need to head west, and I'm not sure the back roads would be any safer. Not to mention, it'll take twice as long to get anywhere." Ben wasn't sure what the answer was here, but he wasn't going to let this interfere with their plans to make camp before dark.

"So what do we do about the truck?" Martin asked.

"Nothing, if we play our cards right. Let's give it a few minutes and then be on our way." Ben didn't know what the Patriot Hooligans were all about, and he really didn't care. He'd be happy if they never saw the red Chevy again. But sitting here all afternoon and trying to decide what to do wouldn't help their cause any. If they wanted to put the Patriot Hooligans' territory behind them quickly, the interstate was their best bet. He had no idea what the PH considered their territory, or where the boundaries were, but he was willing to bet that if he and the others could put in a good hour behind the wheel, they'd be out of trouble. How big could a local gang of extremists be? Another question he was reluctant to guess the answer to.

They waited behind the remains of the gas station for close to fifteen minutes before Ben's impatience got the best of him. In his opinion, there was a point where waiting around any longer was asking for just as much trouble as following the Chevy too closely. For all they knew, another truck could cruise by at any second. It was time to get back on the road.

He wanted to keep the vehicles in the same sequence, Joel up front and him in the rear. But he did ask everyone to do their best and tighten up the gap between vehicles. If Joel ran into trouble, Ben didn't want to find himself a couple of hundred yards back from the front of the convoy. With the way Rita had been falling back and then catching up, only to drift back again, it was a real concern. More than a few times today on the interstate, he'd found himself much farther away from the Jeep than he was comfortable with.

Ben struggled with the idea of asking Allie to drive the Toyota for the rest of the day. But the advantages of having Allie behind the wheel were too attractive to ignore, speed being the biggest one, especially right now, when moving through this area as fast as possible was their best bet to avoid this gang.

Ben discussed it with Sandy first. After all, it was her daughter who would be riding with a stranger. Ben figured Allie could drive the Toyota and Rita would ride passenger. Carlos could ride in the Jeep with Joel and Brad. That put his boys with a stranger as well, but Carlos was pretty harmless in his weakened condition. Besides, Joel had Brad and Gunner as backup. He was sure his concerns were needless to begin with, though. The couple had been nothing but nice and cooperative, and they had nothing to gain by not going along with the current plan.

Sandy was receptive to the idea and surprised Ben by taking the reins and working out the details with her daughter and Rita. Joel looked less than pleased with the arrangement, but Rita looked overjoyed to be relieved of the responsibility.

Once they were back on the interstate, the difference that changing drivers had made was apparent immediately. Ben found himself constantly checking the speedometer to make sure the reading wasn't a figment of his imagination. For the first time on their trip, he was routinely seeing the needle push past sixty miles per hour. He didn't want to get his hopes up, but if they could maintain this pace, they'd reach Little Yankee Run ahead of schedule. Again he wondered if they should push farther but decided that sticking with the plan was best.

Ben half expected to see the big red Chevy every time they passed an exit or came around a curve in the road, but they never did. In fact, they didn't see anyone for the rest of the afternoon, and that was fine with him. They did spot a few more signs and overpasses tagged with the Patriot Hooligans' mark, but that was the worst of it.

The biggest issue they had to deal with was making sure the Scout had enough gas to reach their destination. Ben wanted all the vehicles to have not just enough gas to make it there but also enough to give them a cushion when they broke camp in the morning. If trouble came their way in the middle of the night or early in the morning, they needed to be able to bug out and go far if the situation warranted it. Going to bed with less than half a tank in the truck would be asking for trouble and, at the least, force them to stop early the next day.

Using the map to estimate how much farther they had to go, Ben signaled the others to pull over briefly when they were about half an hour away from what he thought was the Little Yankee Run area. He wanted to check in with everyone and get an idea of where they all stood in terms of needing fuel. They'd been running hard for over three hours now, and as Ben slid out of the Blazer and approached Martin, he tried to mentally prepare for the bad news. He'd been hanging onto the idea that they might reach tonight's campsite without having to stop for gas again.

Martin greeted him with a smile, his left arm hanging out the Scout's window. "Man, we're making good time today, huh?"

Ben nodded. "That we are. I almost hate to ask how you're doing on gas."

Martin checked the gauge. "Not too bad, actually. I got half a tank still."

Ben didn't believe him and leaned in to see for himself. "Wow, I expected you to be down below a quarter tank by now. I hope the gauge is working."

"It's been steady. I mean, it's not jumping around or anything." Martin shrugged.

"All right, let me check with the others, then. I'll let you know the plan on my way back by." Ben smacked the side of the truck lightly with the road atlas as he walked away. That was much better news than he'd anticipated.

"Hey, guys. How're you doing on gas?" Ben stopped outside the driver's side window of the Toyota to talk to Allie.

"Oh, we're good. We're not fast, but we're good." Allie glanced at Rita and smiled. "We're just under three-quarters."

"Are you kidding me? We're making great time

this afternoon. I think we're maybe fifteen minutes or so from the creek. You're doing great, Allie."

"Thanks. So are we stopping for gas or can we make it?"

"I think we're gonna push through and wait to get gas tomorrow. I'll let you know for sure in a sec." Ben continued on up the line of vehicles at a quickened pace, energized by the thought of being able to finish the day's driving sooner than he expected. He knew Joel had enough gas to skip a stop, but he wanted him to have the map since he'd be leading the group to the campsite. His son was leaning out of his window when he arrived at the Jeep.

"Here you go." Ben handed him the road atlas. "Lead us to camp. You're doing a good job, by the way." He reached into the back of the Jeep and messed up Brad's hair before starting for the Blazer.

"Nobody needs to stop?" Joel asked.

"Nope, we're good to go." Ben was well on his way but heard an excited "yes" from both of the boys.

"Follow Joel." Ben smiled as he passed Rita and Allie. If the creek panned out and they found a decent place to set up camp, this could be a good night. He was looking forward to sleeping in the woods.

"I'll see you at camp," Ben said as he passed the Scout.

"You got it," Martin answered.

Once back in the Blazer, he informed the girls that they were heading straight to the creek, no stops. Ben expected Emma to be more excited about not having to be cooped up inside the truck for much longer, but she seemed indifferent.

"I hope you can sleep tonight." Ben was worried that she'd napped too much today and would be up all night.

She sighed. "I'm fine."

Not that it mattered. She wasn't driving, just entertaining the dogs. But he was worried about her nonetheless. Off and on today, she hadn't been feeling well, and she'd also been acting a bit distant, even for a sometimes self-absorbed preteen. He'd make sure to spend some time with her later, one on one. She might not tell him if something were bothering her in front of Sandy.

"It'll be nice to get out of the truck and stay put for a while." Sandy leaned into the breeze coming through her window.

"I'll be happy if the creek has clean water." Ben knew they were still a little ways from kicking their feet up by any means. The creek might turn out to be a bust. They could have more driving ahead of them, but he'd keep that thought to himself until they reached Little Yankee Run and saw the place for themselves.

· 27 ·

It only took another ten minutes of driving before the Scout's brake lights began to glow and the truck merged right. Ben saw the Jeep up ahead as it led the pack off the interstate and down a grass-covered embankment.

"This is it. I'm gonna make a trail down to the creek and then follow a dirt road I see. It looks like it runs upstream a ways. Over," Joel announced over the radio.

"Sounds good. We'll be right behind you after we cover the trail. Over." Ben wanted to make sure the tire tracks through the tall grass weren't obvious to any passing traffic, like he and Joel had done before. It took a little more effort this time to camouflage their trail, especially with four vehicles running over the same spot and matting down the weeds. But Sandy helped him, and after a few minutes, they had the grass propped back up and managed to find a couple of dead branches to mix in.

Sandy stood back and looked from the shoulder. "Looks pretty good. You'd never know four trucks went this way."

"Good. That's the idea." Ben joined her briefly and inspected their work for himself before noticing how far they'd fallen behind the rest of the group. The other trucks had reached the bottom of the ravine and were traveling upstream along the dirt road. He watched the taillights disappear one by one into the woods as they drove. Ben heard the radio sound off from inside the Blazer.

"We better catch up to the others." He looked up and down the interstate one more time and then headed for the truck. The dogs were plenty excited about the prospect of setting up camp, but Emma was absent from the commotion in the truck. "You think Em's all right?"

"She is quiet today, but I can't say I blame her. I'm mean, we're not exactly on vacation here, are we?" Sandy laughed. "Plus, she's not feeling well. I can see it."

"No, I guess you're right, and it's been a pretty rough day. No tougher than the last few, but that isn't much of a consolation," Ben agreed.

"You know she's also at that age, Ben. This can be a tough time for girls, and that's without all this going on. Add in the fact that she doesn't have her mother here to talk to. That's got to be hard on her." Sandy spoke softly as they paused near the back of the truck.

"Yeah, it does. I worry about all of them in that regard," Ben said.

"The same for me with Allie's dad. I feel bad for all of them. I'll try to get her alone later. Maybe she'll open up a little for me," Sandy offered.

"Thanks. I'm gonna do the same after we get camp set up. Maybe between us we can figure out what's going on." It eased Ben's mind a little to know that Sandy was willing to help out in that way. Not that he expected anything less, but it was reassuring.

"Dad, come in. Over." Joel's voice came over the radio again, and Ben rushed to answer the call this time.

"Go ahead. Sorry, just finishing up here. Over."

"The creek looks good. The water is nice and clean. I just wanted to let you know I think this place is gonna work out. Over," Joel reported.

"Great. We'll join you guys shortly. Over." Ben waited for Sandy to close her door before putting the truck in gear and heading down the hill. For the first time today, he didn't feel like he was in a hurry. He was also relieved to hear that the water quality was good; the chances of discovering a polluted stream when they arrived here had plagued his thoughts all day.

He looked at Sandy and then back at Emma with a smile on his face. "Sounds like we found a good spot."

Sandy smiled back, but Emma was once again under the sleeping bag with just her head sticking out far enough to look out the window.

"That's good," she said flatly. At least she had responded. That was more than he'd heard from her during his many other attempts to converse with her today.

Ben tried not to dwell on it too long and put his efforts into smoothly transitioning from the steep grassy slope to the trail running along the creek. He glanced to his left and followed the dirt road with his eyes until it disappeared under the bridge. Then he steered to the right and headed upstream after the others, following the nearly overgrown trail down to a point where it paralleled the creek. Joel was right: the water looked good. Colorado good. Even the dogs were excited, and both of them had migrated to the far side of the rear seat on Ben's side of the truck. Sam and Bajer jockeyed for position in the open window, and Ben could hear their heavy sniffing as they took in the new smells.

"This is really nice down here." Sandy admired their surroundings.

"It is. I'm looking forward to setting up camp," Ben replied. He was, too; this was one of the nicer places they had stopped so far, and it reminded him of Hermosa creek back home, minus the occasional beaver dam. It didn't hurt that the trees and vegetation along the twenty- to thirty-foot-wide creek were green and lush. Compared to the half-dead trees and weeds growing along the interstate, it felt like a small slice of paradise far removed from the world they left back on the highway.

After a few minutes of bumping along the rock-strewn trail, they caught sight of the others. The vehicles were parked in a semicircle around the perimeter of a small clearing near the water's edge. It had obviously been used as a campsite before, but from the looks of things, it had been some time since the place had seen any activity. The trail continued farther into the woods, but it was in worse shape than the section they had just driven, and it veered to the right, away from the water.

Joel, Allie, and Brad met them as they pulled in behind the Scout and completed the horseshoe-shaped string of trucks. Brad had Gunner by the collar and was doing his best to hold him back from greeting the Blazer before Ben had a chance to park.

"What do you think?" Joel asked.

"It's a good spot. We're far enough from the road, I think." Ben looked back in the direction of the interstate. From here, you'd never know the four-lane highway was even there. But it was close enough that Ben thought he could hear a passing car cross the bridge if someone came by during the night.

Martin came stomping out of the woods. "So we're staying here? We can unload our stuff?"

"Well, I guess that's the bathroom over there," Brad joked.

"Sorry, I couldn't hold it anymore," Martin confessed.

"Yeah, we're staying. Let's set up camp and get settled in. Good job getting us here, Joel." Ben patted his son on the shoulder on his way to the creek.

Joel followed him. "It looks pretty good. I'm sure there are trout in there. The water feels nice and cool."

Ben stopped at the water's edge and studied the brisk current for a moment. He knew that was Joel's way of asking if they could go fishing. "After you and your brother set up your tents, help unpack the supplies we need. Got it?"

"Yes, sir." Joel smiled as he turned toward the truck.

"Hey, try to include your sister, will ya? I think she's having a hard time dealing with things right now. Plus, she's had a rough day. Motion sickness, I think," Ben said.

Joel kept walking. "I'll try, but she probably won't want to come."

"Maybe if Allie asked her," Ben added.

"Okay." Joel quickened his pace.

Ben turned back toward the creek and took it in

for a minute. The current was swift, and the sounds of it weaving through the rocks would make for good sleeping tonight. It would also impair the dogs' ability to pick up on approaching footsteps to some degree, but that was the price they had to pay for the convenience of camping near water. They would be able to leave here tomorrow with their water containers full and cold, and that was worth a lot.

The water was knee-deep at most, at least through the section of stream that ran past the campsite. Ben noticed a large riffle above the camp and figured the trucks could ford the creek there if they had to. He wasn't planning on having to do that, but it never hurt to have options when it came to leaving a place. Their experiences had been proven on more than one occasion in their travels.

His solitude didn't last long. Rita and Carlos approached him. It was hard to tell which one of them was helping the other maneuver over the loose rocks along the bank.

"How are you guys doing?" Ben asked.

"Oh, we're great, Ben. This looks like a lovely place," Rita answered.

"Yeah, I think it'll work out well for us."

Carlos let go of his wife and stood up straight. "Listen, Ben, we just wanted to thank you again for helping us get out of that place and get to our daughter's. I know you guys have your own places to go, so we really appreciate it. And we want you to know there is room for you there at her place in Fort Wayne if you want to join us for a day or two and rest up."

"Well, I appreciate the offer. It's tempting, and we might take you up on it if things don't work out for us in Cloverdale. But there's a guy there I owe for saving our butts on the way east."

"We understand. Just know the offer stands." Carlos took his wife's elbow and led her back toward the camp. "We're going to get our tent set up. We'll talk later."

"All right." Ben waved at the couple. The offer to join them at their daughter's was a generous one, for sure, and a good backup. He wasn't sure what gave them the confidence to think that their daughter's place was still there or that she was still alive. But due to their unwavering certainty that all was well in Fort Wayne, he'd started to believe it, too.

Part of him wondered if the offer to travel with them to Fort Wayne was an attempt to ensure they had an escort there. He didn't believe it was, though, based on what he knew of the couple, and he thought it was a genuine gesture of kindness. That made it even harder to stomach the thought of sending them off on their own tomorrow.

Left to fend for themselves, Rita and Carlos wouldn't stand a chance against the likes of the trouble they'd faced today. The only encouraging thing was that they'd be sent on their way with a full tank of gas, and in the Toyota, they'd be able to get to their daughter's without having to stop. But that was poor consolation for the guilt he was starting to feel. It would have been much easier on his conscience if they weren't so nice.

· 28 ·

Ben forced himself to walk away from the creek. He could have stayed there for much longer, lost in his thoughts and the rushing water. He was tired, and although it wouldn't be dark for a while, the sun was already casting a shadow over the campsite. There'd be plenty of time to feel guilty tomorrow.

Right now, he was going to set up his tent and start a small fire. With any luck, he could talk Emma into helping him, assuming she didn't tag along with her brothers on their attempt to catch fish. He was hoping she would join them, but if not, he'd keep her busy. Too much sitting and thinking was no good. And if he could spend some time alone with her, maybe he could figure out what was bothering her the most. He wasn't sure if he could help, but he had to try. It hurt him to see his daughter so troubled.

After the day they'd had, Ben wouldn't normally be up to making a fire and taking the added risk of giving away their location, but there was no denying the morale it would generate. He also didn't want to risk any more animal encounters. A campfire didn't guarantee being left alone by any late-night four-legged visitors, but it was a good deterrent. And with the amount of dry wood available in the woods beyond the creek, the fire should burn fairly cleanly using the two-hole method.

"We're done with the tents and we even helped Rita and Carlos set up theirs." Joel didn't have to ask; Ben knew what they wanted permission to do.

"Go ahead. Take the radio and flashlights." Ben wanted to add about ten more warnings to his instructions but stopped himself. They knew the rest, anyway: be careful, don't take chances, take your weapons.

"We'll try to be back before it gets dark." Joel began setting up the rods.

"Anyone else going with you?" Ben asked.

"Allie might."

"What about your sister?" Ben was afraid he knew the answer to that question already.

"She said she didn't feel like it." Joel handed one of the rods to his brother. "I'm not going to beg her. Besides, she said she'd keep the dogs here. That way, we can actually catch something."

"All right, go ahead." Ben sighed. "And good luck." It wasn't the boy's fault Emma didn't want to join him and Allie, and it wasn't their responsibility, either. It was equally important for Joel, Allie, and Brad to have a little fun. They had more than earned it today.

"Do you mind, Mom?" Allie asked.

"No, have fun. Rita and I can handle dinner." Sandy dragged one of the five-gallon water containers to the edge of the tailgate.

"I'll give you a hand after I get the fire going," Ben offered. "Hey, Em, want to help me gather some wood?"

"I'll help with that," Martin said. That wasn't what Ben wanted, but at least the guy was willing to help.

"I kind of have a headache." Emma was sitting half in, half out of her tent with the flap thrown back. Her legs stuck out onto a blanket she was sharing with all three of the dogs.

"I'll get you something for that." Sandy started rummaging through the back of the Blazer. "You two go ahead. Us girls will be fine." She winked at Ben and returned to her search for the first-aid bag. Maybe she could get through to Emma. Ben stuck the shovel in the ground and stood up to brush the dirt off his knees.

"All right then. We'll be right back. Come on, Martin." Ben grabbed the hatchet from the Blazer.

"Thanks," he whispered to Sandy. She nodded, and he and Martin headed for a section of woods away from the creek, where they would have more luck finding dry wood to burn. They hauled several loads of firewood into the camp until they had what Ben thought was enough to last them through the night. He finished digging out the firepit and within minutes had a nice little fire crackling away.

Joel, Brad, and Allie returned from fishing sooner than expected with a stringer full of rainbow trout and one brown trout. Brad eagerly let everyone know he'd caught the largest rainbow. Ben helped Sandy and Rita prepare the fish, and they all sat down for a good meal around the fire. The topic of conversation varied, but no one mentioned any of the problems they encountered today. It seemed as though they were all eager to forget about life beyond the flickering light of the fire, or at least ignore it for the time being.

As they all prepared for bed, Ben was able to have a word with Sandy and see if she'd had any luck talking to Emma. Unfortunately, she hadn't, and it was too late for Ben to try now. Emma had been quick to wash up after dinner so she could go to bed early. She said she still wasn't feeling well, and after feeding Bajer her leftovers, the two of them disappeared into her tent.

The others were fading fast as well, and they started slowly disappearing from around the campfire.

Ben loaded the firepit with wood and asked Joel to do the same before calling it a night. He cautioned them about staying up too late and bid them goodnight before brushing his teeth and climbing into his tent. The kids were welcome to stay up longer if they wanted, but he was anxious to get off his feet.

It was going to feel good to lie down, and as he zipped the fly closed, he felt his eyes growing heavy. Sleep would come quickly for him tonight, and he figured it was a good idea to take the time now and make sure the KSG was handy and ready for use. Once that was done and his pistol was tucked under his pillow, it wasn't hard to tune the world out and drift off to the rhythm of the rushing water.

Ben woke up once during the night, but he only stayed awake long enough to take a quick look around the camp and throw a few logs on the fire before crawling back into his sleeping bag. Morning arrived well before it seemed possible, and coffee became Ben's main priority after he worked the kinks out of his back. The night was uneventful, and he was thankful for that.

The woods were quiet in the early moments of dawn, and with everyone still sleeping, he did his best not to make any noise when he moved about the camp. As soon as the coffee was ready, he poured a cup and slipped away to the water's edge, where he found a suitable rock to sit on and enjoy the stillness of the morning.

His peace and quiet was short-lived, though, and either the smell of the coffee or the light of the rising sun prompted the others from their tents one by one.

"Good morning." Sandy sat on a nearby rock.

"Morning." Ben watched as Gunner waded into the creek just far enough to take in a few sloppy mouthfuls of water. Joel and Allie were up and moving around the Blazer, while Brad struggled to fight his desire to go back to bed.

"It was a good spot after all." Sandy held up her cup.

Ben nodded. "Yes, a welcome change."

"Should I make more?" Martin appeared out of nowhere, shaking the empty coffee pot in front of him.

"Yes, please. Would you? I'd really like some more," Sandy said, sending Martin straight back toward the camp. "You don't look like you're ready for him yet. "She laughed.

"Thanks." Ben tipped his cup back at her. She was right; the morning was too nice to ruin with empty, pointless chatter. Maybe he'd feel differently after another cup of coffee, but he doubted that very much. Looking back toward the camp, he swept from right to left in search of his daughter. She wasn't up yet, or at least not among those walking around and making breakfast. Even Rita and Carlos were outside their tent and tidying up.

"Go ahead," Sandy said.

"Is it that obvious?" Ben smiled.

"Yes. Now go check on your daughter," she joked.

Ben swallowed the last of his coffee and headed for Emma's tent. But before he could get there, he heard the zipper slide. Bajer darted out of the opening and relieved herself in some nearby bushes. He froze for a second and debated whether he should try to sneak away or greet his daughter. He didn't want her to know he was about to check on her and wake her up. That wasn't how he wanted to start the day with her. It was hard enough to get her to talk to him without her feeling like he didn't trust her enough to get up on her own.

"Good morning." Ben had no choice but to stay put and greet her when her head popped out of the opening and she spotted him.

"Hey." Emma rubbed her eyes as she struggled to adjust to the sunlight in her face.

"How are you feeling?" Ben asked.

"Hot." She cleared her throat and started to stand up. "Ow, oh...oh...that hurts." She winced and dropped back to the ground.

"What is it?" Ben asked.

Emma held up her left foot and inspected it, but Ben could see the puffy red cut on her heel from where he was standing. All of a sudden, Rita was by his side and then just as quickly kneeling next to his daughter.

"Can I take a look at that?" She took Emma's foot in her hand and held it up in the sun.

"Ah, that hurts." Emma sucked in air sharply through her teeth.

"I'm sorry, honey. We need to get this cleaned out. Where did you get this?"

"Back at the motel yesterday morning when we were loading the trucks in the water. I thought it was just a little cut...and there was so much going on. I guess I forgot to say anything about it." Emma winced again as Rita turned her foot and inspected the other side.

Ben turned to go and get the first-aid kit, but Allie was only a few steps away and had the bright orange bag in her hand.

"Here." She passed the kit to Rita. "What do we need?"

"Let's see." Rita rifled through the bag. "No... no...here. Can I get some filtered water?"

Joel rushed in with his Nalgene and handed it over right away. Rita didn't hesitate and went to work, using several packets from the first-aid kit while warning Emma occasionally that this would hurt a little. She finished up by wrapping the wound in clean white gauze and instructing Emma to stay off her foot and drink plenty of water.

Ben felt useless as he stood still and watched. The day had been so crazy and fast-paced that he didn't even notice his own daughter was in pain.

He crouched next to her. "Are you okay?"

"I'll be okay. It just hurts right now."

"All right, well, you sit tight. We'll break down your tent for you. I just want you to eat breakfast and take it easy, okay?"

She nodded and did her best to hide the pain.

"Can I talk to you, Ben?" Rita headed toward the stream, only looking back to make sure he was following. She stopped when they were out of earshot of the others. "She has an infection, and it's only going to get worse unless we get some antibiotics in her."

Sandy joined them and stood next to Ben as Rita delivered the bad news.

"She's right. The foot is pretty swollen, and it happened fast if that cut's from yesterday morning," Sandy added.

"Don't we have anything in the first-aid kit?" He knew they didn't, but he was at a loss for words right now. An antibiotic was going to be hard to come by. Every pharmacy and hospital from here to Colorado had been picked clean by looters. Reese had some medications back in Cloverdale. She'd given Gunner an antibiotic for his paw, but that was a long shot.

"My daughter is a doctor. She runs a small practice in Fort Wayne. She could help us. I know she'll have the antibiotics Emma needs," Rita stated.

"We don't even know if your daughter is still

alive." Ben was immediately embarrassed by his outburst, but he could feel the desperation creeping in. Emma needed help, and their options were few.

Rita looked Ben dead in the eyes. "She's there. I know she is. Julia and Edward are survivors. They were prepared for a world like this."

"Fort Wayne is closer than Cloverdale," Sandy said.

"But we don't know what we'll find in Fort Wayne," Ben argued.

"And we don't know what we'll find in Cloverdale, either. It's a roll of the dice either way. At least if Rita's daughter can't help, we can continue on to Cloverdale from there without backtracking," Sandy reasoned.

She was right, and Ben couldn't think of any more reasons to argue against the plan.

"Please, trust me," Rita pleaded.

Ben couldn't believe how fast things had changed. He was just enjoying his coffee and imagining him and the others driving through the wall of cars surrounding Cloverdale sometime late tonight or early tomorrow morning. Now Emma's life was in danger and they had plotted a new course within seconds.

Ben nodded slowly. "Better tell the others we're headed to Fort Wayne."

Find out about Bruno Miller's next book by signing
up for his newsletter:
http://brunomillerauthor.com/sign-up/

No spam, no junk, just news (sales, freebies, and
releases). Scouts honor.

Enjoy the book?
Help the series grow by telling a friend about it
and taking the time to leave a review.

BOOKS BY BRUNO MILLER

THE DARK ROAD SERIES:
Breakdown
Escape
Resistance
Fallout
Extraction
Reckoning
Deception
Restitution
Desperation

CLOVERDALE SERIES:
Impact
Survival
Endurance
Confrontation

ABOUT THE AUTHOR

BRUNO MILLER is the author of the Dark Road series. He's a military vet who likes to spend his downtime hanging out with his wife and kids, or getting in some range time. He believes in being prepared for any situation.

http://brunomillerauthor.com/

https://www.facebook.com/BrunoMillerAuthor/

https://www.instagram.com/brunomillerauthor/

Made in the USA
Las Vegas, NV
15 March 2021